LADY MARIANNE AND THE CAPTAIN

THE SEDGEWICK LADIES
BOOK III

ISABELLA THORNE

Mikita Associates

COPYRIGHT

Copyright © 2023 by Isabella Thorne

All rights reserved.

No part of this book may be reproduced in any form or by any electronic or mechanical means, including information storage and retrieval systems, without written permission from the author, except for the use of brief quotations in a book review.

PART I

CHAPTER 1

Lady Marianne Sedgewick, the middle daughter of the Earl of Ashbury jolted guiltily at the sound of footsteps in the corridor just beyond the library. Judging by the shadows lengthening on the lawn, visible from the large window that graced her favored nook in the book-filled sanctuary, a great deal more than five minutes of time had passed since she had picked up a heavy volume for 'just a moment'. Of course, the siren's song of information had been more of a temptation than she could overcome. She had known perfectly well that it would be so and now had no one but herself to blame if she was caught late and unprepared to entertain her father's guests.

Unprepared might be an understatement, she realized with growing dismay. She had at least had the sense to dress for dinner before slipping into the library, but had failed to realize that the prized leather-bound volume was coated rather thickly with decades' worth of accumulated dust and grime which was now smeared liberally across the front of her once-spotless white muslin gown.

"Oh, for Heaven's sake," she murmured, still setting the book aside with the gentleness and care that its advanced age merited, regardless of her ill temper. Marianne could hardly think of a worse time for such a thing to occur. Her elder sister, Arabella, had played the role of hostess for their father ever since their mother's untimely demise years ago, but Arabella, now a baroness, the Right Honorable Lady Willingham, was no longer available for the task. Lord Sedgewick had undoubtedly taken Arabella's skill and hard work for granted, and Marianne knew she was nearly as guilty of doing he same thing herself. Arabella had always indulged her preference for studying - and her distaste for conventional, stilted conversations, which had always struck Marianne as being impossibly pointless and dull.

She had assured Arabella dozens of times that she was perfectly able to take up the mantle of hostess. After all, how hard could it be? She had said. There was a housekeeper to assign work to the maids and to ensure the rooms were ready, and the kitchen steward to see to the buying of the food. A cook and scullery maids prepared the feast. Footmen served it. With so many involved in the ordering of the evening, it didn't seem that Marianne had much to do at all, but that statement was far from accurate.

As hostess, she had the last word on all of it, and even with the servants' help, she could not shirk her duty, and she could not call upon her sister. First of all, it would be the height of embarrassment that a person of her status and intellect could not host a simple party, and secondly, Arabella was simply not available. It really did not matter if she were up to the task or not, Marianne had determined. It would have been the height of selfishness to do anything to keep Arabella from marrying the unlikely, yet undeniable love of her life. Marianne had kept her worry about entertaining to herself.

This party and all subsequent parties in her father's house were Marianne's responsibility. After all, she could not leave the task to Daphne. Her youngest sister would likely let the party goers fend for themselves while she went off on some adventure. The thought brought a wry smile to her lips and a welcome feeling of mirth to her heart.

Everything had felt dismal and strange since Arabella's wedding a fortnight ago. Marianne had been forced to acknowledge that her sister Arabella, now Lady Willingham, really - *that* would take a great deal longer than a mere fortnight to become accustomed to- had done a deal of unseen work to keep the household running smoothly.

Marianne had actually had only the barest surface knowledge of everything involved in such an undertaking. However, she was not considered one of the brightest young women in England for nothing, she had told both herself and her father when he had dubiously informed her that he would be having guests to dinner that evening. She would simply apply her substantial intellect to the problems at hand and everything would work out splendidly.

It *had*, too, until she had made the critical mistake of congratulating herself on how seamlessly the arrangements for the evening had come together. She had not even consulted Arabella once. Not that consulting Arabella was an option, as she was still away on her honeymoon trip, but the point, of course, was that Marianne had not needed to do so. Everything had been ready perfectly, with time to spare, and like a fool, she had decided to reward herself with a few moments' solitude in the library. It had been sheer hubris, and anyone who had studied the classics as much as Marianne knew the inevitable consequences of hubris. It was a lesson learned in innumerable classics.

"So much for all of my claims that we can learn to avoid mistakes by reading about other people committing them in stories. I am every bit as bad as Odysseus, after all, in thought if not in deed. Of course, his solution for unwanted guests was a bit extreme, in slaughtering them, but one begins to see his point…" Marianne's wry soliloquy faded away as she began, unbidden, to picture the various ramifications of a civilized English host adopting the Greek hero's approach to such a problem, or conversely, how different the story might have been, had Odysseus been the one trapped at home all of those years rather than Penelope. The thought made her giggle. Odysseus certainly would not have put up with guests abusing his servants and sleeping with the maids. No, she thought. Those guests would have met their end on the tip of Odysseus' sword, which right now, did not sound like a terrible idea at all.

The louder rumblings of voices in the corridor brought Marianne to the present moment *again*, and she shook herself with irritation as she realized that she had wasted still more time wool gathering. Wiping frantically at the dusty smudges on her gown had only made them worse, but there was no way that she could admit defeat quite so early in her foray as a hostess. Thinking quickly, Marianne decided that the most practical course of action would be to slip out of the library undetected, change her gown as quickly as possible, and be introduced to the earl's guests a few minutes late, but decently attired, at least. She was not one to primp and dawdle. She could dress quickly.

Of course, that brought up the problem of *how* to slip away undetected, since the guests were evidently at the very threshold of the library. Indeed, the heavy iron handle of the doors began turning before she could so much as take a step. To her utter horror, the cheerfully handsome face of the dashing Captain Andrew Larkin appeared in the doorway. He was glancing carelessly back at his companions and continuing some conversation with them even as he partially opened the door.

Mortification rolled over Marianne in waves. Of all the gentlemen in the world, why did it have to be *him* to catch her in such a state? She ordered herself firmly to set that emotion aside for the time being. Waving frantically and silently, she succeeded in catching the captain's attention before he fully entered the library, and to her relief, he paused in the doorway at the sight of her.

He was a tall, imposing figure, taking up the whole of the doorway. His broad shoulders had the added effect of blocking the other guests from view.

But it was not his handsome countenance that made Lady Marianne suddenly feel her heart race, nor the sight of his muscular frame beneath the fine uniform that made her flush with modesty. It was instead the way he moved. He moved with the effortless grace of a man in full control of himself, while the quiet confidence in his voice spoke of both his wisdom and his courage. He seemed to fill the room with his presence.

Marianne did her very best to convey, without words, the quandary in which she found herself, by gesturing frantically at her besmirched gown. To his credit, Captain Larkin seemed to catch on almost at once. Giving her a conspiratorial, and decidedly cheeky wink, he began backing out of the doorway, saying in a hardy and convincing voice, that he had not yet returned the last book he borrowed from the earl's library, and he dared not enter the premises with such a crime on his conscience.

To Marianne's relief, the rest of the guests seemed to accept this statement without question. Such was the unconscious air of authority the captain possessed, she supposed. She had noticed, that in general, men automatically followed Captain Larkin's lead. The party could be heard making its way further down the corridor. Waiting as short an amount of time as she dared, Marianne slipped noiselessly out of the library and dashed in the opposite direction from the retreating backs of her guests.

She took the stairs two at a time, in a most unladylike haste. She was sure the racing of her heart was not due to the chance encounter with Captain Larkin, but only due to her swift retreat. She did not pause for a moment to consider, but instead burst into her chamber so abruptly that her maid had to stifle a shriek.

"My lady, whatever have you done to that gown?" Philippa demanded, setting aside her own rattled nerves for the moment as she took in the crisis at hand. "To say nothing of your hair."

"What *have* I done to my hair?" wondered Marianne, momentarily distracted from her urgent mission. For the life of her, she could not recall so much as touching the artistic arrangement that Philippa had toiled with so painstakingly. Peering into her looking glass, however, Marianne could see that the once-elegant blonde coif was hopelessly disheveled, scarcely even a shadow of its former gleamingly sleek perfection. "Heavens," she muttered.

"I daresay you've run your fingers through it whilst thinking about some puzzle or translation or some such thing. I recognize the mess right enough. And I recognize the stain on your poor gown, too, it's the grime from one of those nasty old books, isn't it?"

Marianne nodded, as with dusty fingers, she pulled her fichu from her shoulders, thinking the first order of business tomorrow was to see that the library was carefully dusted, but right now, she had other problems.

"Well, it *is from a book,*" she said to Philippa, "but I cannot really spare any time to be scolded for it just now. I have only just barely avoided being seen in such a state by Father's guests, and I'm frightfully late to meet them as it is."

"Come here, then, and let me put you to rights," Philippa relented, with a resigned shake of her head. "It isn't as though I haven't had plenty of practice doing such a thing in a hurry, not in this house. If it isn't you getting lost in some book and forgetting the time, it's Miss Daphne climbing a tree or getting into a mud-puddle battle, or trying to ride a cow."

"A cow?" Marianne repeated while the maid pulled loose the ribbons at her bodice. She had not heard that particular story of her younger sister's escapades, but the maid did not elaborate. She went right on with her gentle tirade.

"And always right at the last moment, before guests arrive or the carriage needs to leave. Although, I will just point out that to my knowledge, Miss Daphne has remained decently attired this evening, and her still mostly a child." She raised an accusing eyebrow at Marianne.

"We are really frightfully lucky to have you, Philippa," said Marianne, her voice muffled from the depths of the muslin gown the maid drew over her head.

"That is true enough, I suppose, although perhaps you would do better with one of those costumers backstage at a theatre or ballet. They have a great deal of skill at changing people over in a few seconds time, I hear," Philippa continued, deftly slipping a clean gown over Marianne's head and fastening it up at a lightning fast pace that would surely have put the most expert of stage dressers to shame.

"I doubt any of them could stand the stress of being ladies' maid to the Sedgewick sisters," Marianne teased affectionately, wriggling as helpfully as she could to seat the dress properly. She handed the ribbon to her maid to tie about her waist. "Not anything as splendidly as you do." Marianne took the moment to re-fasten the button of the fichu at her neck and seat it properly over her bosom.

"Not unless they'd also had a bit of experience taming lions or ordering pirates about, they wouldn't," Philippa agreed, giving Marianne a fond smile before attacking her hair with a handful of pins.

CHAPTER 2

Captain Andrew Larkin, looking thoroughly relaxed and fit, surveyed the elegant drawing room as he idled some way behind the rest of the gentlemen. It was his leisurely air of contentment that drew Marianne's notice, she supposed, since he appeared to be the perfect opposite of how she was feeling herself. Another moment's reflection made her revise that opinion, however. Examined objectively, it was undeniable that the captain's presence usually commanded her attention whenever he was in a room. Certainly, he was a well-favored looking personage, she thought frankly. Tall, strong and handsome, he was the very ideal image of a heroic soldier, with the commendations to prove it.

There was more to it than the bold, level gaze of his blue eyes and the careless fall of his dark brown locks, though. It was something about his very presence that seemed to strike more people than just Marianne.

Indeed, lingering behind the others as they made their way from their after-dinner port and gentlemanly discussions to the feminine company gathered in the drawing room, Captain Larkin had only managed to emphasize the impact of his presence. He was in more ways than one, head and shoulders above the others.

"Ah, there *is* something fascinating about a military gentleman, isn't there, my dear?" asked Mrs. Millworth in a conspiratorial aside, seeming to notice Marianne's distraction. Marianne took no offense at the implication, particularly as Mrs. Millworth was a long-cherished friend of the Sedgewick family and had stood in for the Sedgewick girls' mother as much as she could.

"I daresay, I ought not appear particularly fascinated," Marianne said with a rueful smile at her companion. "Someone less charitable and understanding than yourself might think that I have designs upon the poor captain, or upon officers in general."

"Well, I'm sure you are not the first woman whose head was turned by a smart uniform, and it would hardly be shocking if you *did* notice the man," Mrs. Millworth pointed out bemusedly. "He is a fine looking, well-born young gentleman who comes with a great many recommendations to both his character and his prospects, and such are few and far between."

"The greatest recommendation to Captain Larkin's prospects, as far as I know, is the great fortune he has in his future sister-in-law," teased Marianne, making Mrs. Millworth laugh merrily. Mrs. Millworth's only daughter, Ellen, was betrothed to Captain Larkin's older brother. Doctor Roger Larkin was perhaps not so dashing and athletic as his brother, but he was nevertheless quite appealing, with his combination of a brilliant mind and innate kindness.

At one time, Marianne, had she reflected on the matter at all, would have thought the gentle, serious doctor an unlikely match for the romantic-minded Ellen Millworth, yet even the most casual observer could see that the pair were perfect for one another. Following Mrs. Millworth's fond gaze, she could see Ellen smiling up at the doctor as he walked toward her, adoration and happiness written clearly on her lovely features. For his part, Doctor Larkin looked as though he were illuminated from within as he beheld his love, so much so that he bore little resemblance to the overworked and weary physician that had cared for their small village so doggedly for some years now.

"I declare, just seeing the pair of them look at one another fills my heart to bursting," Mrs. Millworth murmured, dashing a single tear away from her eye. "There was a time I despaired of ever seeing my sweet girl ever truly happy again, and now just look at her."

"She appears to be happier than ever, if such a thing is even possible," agreed Marianne. Ellen had always been a singularly lighthearted creature, living what seemed to be a charmed existence until very recently. Her unfortunate engagement of the previous summer had resulted in a very dark time for Ellen, but those days seemed to be entirely behind her.

"I cannot tell you who is more anxious for their wedding day, Ellen, or dear Roger. I admit to feeling rather impatient myself at times, although I know perfectly well I shall weep dreadfully when it really comes down to it."

"When is the wedding to be?" Marianne asked, realizing that in the bustle of preparing for Arabella's wedding and subsequent departure, she had not actually asked the date of Ellen's nuptials.

"Ah, well, not for several months yet, I am afraid," Mrs. Millworth sighed, shaking her head a little. "Roger's mother is determined to have all of her family present for the occasion, which is, of course, understandable. She has a rather large family and has not had them all in one place for some time, so this is her chance. Two of the elder sons are abroad on business and evidently cannot possibly return any sooner than early spring. Andrew, there, will be staying here until the wedding, and I very much doubt if he has stayed in such a tame place for so long since he began his commission."

"Indeed," murmured Marianne, rather pointlessly. She was not generally given to such inanities in conversation, but Mrs. Millworth's news had taken her rather by surprise. She had assumed that Captain Larkin would be departing for his next military post within a matter of days, although she could not imagine what difference his remaining would make to her. Nonetheless, her heart fluttered in a most unaccustomed way. "I beg your pardon, Mrs. Millworth, but I suppose I had better get on with my duties as hostess and speak with the other guests, hadn't I?"

"Be very brave," Mrs. Millworth laughed, knowing quite well how little Marianne cared for such social interactions.

Marianne thought she did well enough for a time, moving systematically from one small knot of guests to another and engaging them in polite conversation. With very strict effort she kept her mind from straying to topics of actual interest, but the combination of that strain and the necessity of continually making sure that her younger sister Daphne did nothing shocking was frankly exhausting.

That was not entirely fair, she supposed. Daphne had made great strides in maturity and manners over the course of the last few months, but being raised by an admittedly distracted father and two sisters scarcely old enough to care for themselves had resulted in some stubborn quirks of Daphne's character. However, she seemed to be on her very best behavior for the evening, which Marianne noted with some relief. Indeed, her performance at the pianoforte was roundly considered to be enchanting.

"Your younger sister is quite an accomplished musician," commented a balding gentleman who had developed the unsettling habit of materializing at Marianne's side several times this evening. She seemed to have her own unsettling habit of forgetting the names of guests she did not revere.

"She has been quite consumed with practicing lately," Marianne replied as agreeably as she could manage. The name completely escaped her. She felt quite the fool.

The man was a guest, after all, and if he was determined to monopolize her time, she would just have to resign herself to such a fate graciously. "But I cannot claim that she has been particularly diligent in developing her talents until very recently. Her instructor claims that she has a natural gift."

"I daresay her instructor is correct in that assessment. Tell me, Lady Marianne, is musical ability a family trait? As delighted as I am to hear your sister's performance, I confess that I should be quite enraptured to hear music that flowed from *your* lovely hands and throat."

"I am afraid that I do not play very well at all, sir," Marianne managed, entirely taken aback by the unexpected and oddly intimate comment. For the life of her, she could not recall the gentleman's name, and searching her memory, she had no idea if she had ever spoken to him before that evening. Surely, they had been introduced. He was an anonymous looking sort of man, average in height, build, and coloring. He possessed no quality that could distinguish him from dozens of other gentlemen, aside from his thinning hair and the discomfiting smile that he was bestowing upon her.

"Ah, such delightfully feminine modesty." he exclaimed, rather more effusively than Marianne could imagine such a comment warranted. "But you must not set your own talents aside for the sake of a younger sister who is not yet out, you know, Lady Marianne. I must insist you grace us with a performance, however, and not allow you to be overshadowed."

"Really, I am not given to displays of false modesty. I have never taken the time or trouble to develop even a rudimentary level of musical ability and any performance of mine would be perfectly dreadful," said Marianne as firmly as she dared.

"I can hardly believe *that*," replied her tormentor insinuatingly, and to her alarm he actually seemed at he point of attempting to draw her towards the pianoforte, looking all the while as though he were doing her a great favor.

CHAPTER 3

"Lady Marianne has always struck me as being remarkably honest. I should take her at her word if I were you, Mr. Baxter," interposed Captain Larkin, coming to Marianne's rescue before she had to decide if avoiding the humiliation of an unskilled performance would be worth the indignity of struggling against the enthusiastic gentleman's insistence.

"Baxley," corrected the other, looking nettled but subsiding nevertheless. *That* was his name Baxley," Marianne noted, feeling slightly less at a disadvantage.

"Of course, my humblest apologies, Mr. Baxley," Captain Larkin said with a polite bow.

"Think nothing of it, Captain. I hate to disagree with you, sir, but perhaps you may be mistaken in your assessment of this situation. After all, you have been absent from the drawing rooms for quite some time. The fine subtleties of young ladies' manners, you know, can often be misunderstood by those who have not spent much time in gentle society. I assure you that it is quite conventional for a lady to protest her own inadequacy in such matters, but really be wonderfully talented and eager to display her skill before company. She only has to be convinced. She *wants* to be convinced."

Marianne took a steadying breath, wondering if the man was always so sure that a woman meant yes, when she said no. It was a disconcerting thought, but she was about to counter it, when Captain Larkin spoke in her defense.

"I confess, I would never have suspected such subterfuge," admitted the captain with a mild and agreeable air. "Tell us, Lady Marianne, if I have stomped all over a delicate social convention with my rough manners, and I shall apologize quite profusely."

"I fear, it is I who have been in ignorance, sir," Marianne returned, doing her best to keep her expression neutral. Between her considerable annoyance at Mr. Baxley's manner, her slight amusement at his indignation, and her unaccountable giddiness at the captain's steady regard, she scarcely knew what her expression might be. "I am perfectly in earnest when I say that I have no musical ability whatsoever, and any performance of mine would be most undesirable for myself as well as for everyone within earshot." A smile played about her lips.

"I beg your pardon most sincerely, Lady Marianne," said Mr. Baxley, his ears and then the pate of his bald head turning a most vivid shade of crimson. So much so, that the blush showed through his pale blond hair. He looked entirely taken aback. "I...I certainly did not mean to cause you any distress with my assumption. Such a refined and accomplished young lady as you...I naturally thought..." he stuttered.

"I fear I am scarcely able to lay claim to the accolade of accomplished. I am decidedly hopeless at nearly every skill encompassed by that description. I have spent almost all of my time, until very recently, engaged in academic pursuits, to the neglect and exclusion of the more feminine arts."

"Indeed? Why that is most, ah, most unique, I must say." Mr. Baxley's horrified expression belied his attempt at diplomacy. "Academic pursuits, you say? What, precisely, does that encompass?" It was clear the man had nothing to say and was forcing the conversation off on her with his open-ended question.

"Oh, a great many disciplines," Marianne confessed, taking the reins. She was unable to conceal her amusement at his discomfiture. She decided she should present herself with systematic vigor. After all, it seemed that this might be a way to discourage the gentleman. "Latin and Greek, of course," she said, ticking the subjects off on her fingers. "And the histories and writings of antiquity. Higher mathematics. I find calculus simply bewitching, don't you?" She gave him a wide-eyed stare which she was certain flummoxed the man entirely as he was enamored of her blond beauty, but completely horrified by her words. "But most recently I have become fascinated by the study of medicine," she added with excess vim and verve. She screwed up her face, as if in thought. "I suppose the poisonings that plagued this area a while ago sparked my interest, particularly since it was Doctor Larkin's knowledge of poisons and antidotes that ultimately led to the apprehension of a murderer." She cast a quick glance at Captain Larkin at the mention of his brother, and realized that was almost a mistake. The captain was barely holding in his own mirth as he hid his smile behind his wine glass. She turned immediately back to Mr. Baxley with renewed enthusiasm.

"Although *that* incident also caused me to be almost equally fascinated with the strange twists and turns of the human mind, naturally enough. What makes a person contemplate murder, do you suppose?"

"I...that is to say, I hardly know," the unfortunate Mr. Baxley stammered. He appeared to have become stuck at her assumption that he would find calculus as bewitching as she did, which caused something of a delay before He realized she was speaking of medicine and murder in a cavalier and matter-of-fact way. "It does not seem *quite* natural, I must say."

"It was a very logical connection, I assure you, Mr. Baxley," interjected Captain Larkin helpfully.

Marianne chanced another glance at the man and saw that he was even more amused at the turn of the conversation than she herself was. He was trying to keep his face serious, but his lips most decidedly twitched as he answered. "We were all taken by surprise at finding that a meek and quiet gentlewoman was not only capable of most cold-blooded acts of murder of her own family members, but indeed seemed utterly without remorse.

Such a discovery, on one's very doorstep, as it were, would naturally cause even a mildly curious mind to wonder at the roots and formation of criminal insanity."

"Perhaps that is so," Mr. Bexley said, "although I daresay that a great many members of polite society would not admit to such curiosity. But it is without question a most indelicate subject for a young lady, I should think. As indeed are the vast majority of the other subjects that Lady Marianne has mentioned just now. I wonder at her being allowed to spend any amount of time whatsoever in such unfeminine pursuits."

Marianne barely registered the insult to herself. She was quite accustomed to people in general, and gentlemen in particular, expressing disapproval at the idea of a woman studying with any seriousness, but it was the sudden change in Captain Larkin' manner that caught her attention. His easy amusement vanished in an instant and the very air around him seemed to hum with energy and menace as he drew himself up and pinned Mr. Baxley with such a fiery gaze that it bordered on assault.

Mr. Baxley took an involuntary step back.

If she did not intervene, Marianne was certain that the captain would almost certainly challenge the foolish man to a duel then and there.

"It has been my great privilege to be afforded sufficient leisure to pursue my studies as much as I wish," she said in an even, soothing voice, which she hoped was directed at Captain Larkin as much as Mr. Baxley. "Daphne and I will be the first to admit that we have been greatly indulged by our father and eldest sister after the death of our mother. It is certainly true that academic subjects are generally considered to be beyond the scope of a lady, but I do not believe I have done anything truly improper by improving my mind. One never knows, however, what great breadth of mischief I might have come to if I were constrained into mental idleness, for such a thing goes against my very nature. I would do better if I were deprived of light or nourishment or shelter than if I were deprived of knowledge and books."

To Marianne's surprise and gratification, Captain Larkin almost instantly seemed to accept that she was capable of defending herself and seemed to imperceptibly stand down.

Mr. Baxley, although he appeared to be oblivious of the brief threat to his bodily safety, looked at Marianne as if she were some sort of rare and dangerous serpent.

"Indeed. That is a most… liberal way of thinking, I suppose. Ah, forgive me, Lady Marianne, Captain Larkin. I see someone I must speak to…" Mr. Baxley trailed off, not even bothering to conclude his flimsy excuse before making his hasty escape.

"Oh dear, I suppose I mismanaged that quite badly," Marianne sighed, although she could not seem to summon any sincere regret. "I am making quite a muddle of this evening all around."

"Not at all, at least not from my perspective," Captain Larkin replied, not bothering to conceal his amusement at the situation. "Unless your intention was to encourage the narrow-minded Mr. Baxley in his idea of pursuing your hand, in which case I fear you *have* mismanaged things. However, I have no doubt that you will be able to salvage matters with him if you wish."

"His idea of pursuing my hand?" Marianne was very rarely struck speechless, but she felt dangerously close to such a phenomenon at the moment. That *would* explain Mr. Baxley's strange manner, she supposed.

"Lady Marianne, surely you noticed he has been following you about all evening like a besotted puppy?"

"I certainly had not noticed any such thing," she contradicted him flatly, forgetting her manners once again. "I have been far too preoccupied with my attempts to keep from failing altogether in my first attempt at stepping into Arabella's role as hostess. I cannot imagine how she did this with such aplomb and ease for so long, and beginning at such a young age, as well. I fear I have sadly underestimated my sister's skills all this time. I am making a muddle of this."

"Perhaps you will permit me to say that from my admittedly limited perspective, the evening has gone remarkably well, and you have been a delightful hostess," Captain Larkin said, taking her hand and bowing over it.

"Thank you for your kind words and your gallant rescue, Captain Larkin, both now and earlier."

Marianne felt a warmth spread through her at his touch. Of course, he was only being polite, but the admiration in his voice was unmistakable. She felt a thrill of anticipation course through her veins as his lips brushed the back of her gloved hand and she felt the heat of a blush warm her face. His deep blue eyes met hers for a moment, and Marianne was sure he shared her momentary surprise at the spark of attraction that had flared between them. He straightened and released her hand, but not before Marianne caught sight of the same spark of emotion in his gaze.

She certainly sported her colors now, but she looked away. Before she did, she noticed that Captain Larkin had not moved. He was studying her as if she were some complicated war campaign he was determined to win, and she recognized the single-minded gaze. She saw it in her own mirror when she was particularly resolute about a project--when it consumed her.

The look of concentration broke, and he smiled at her. That smile lit her world. "I particularly admire your gown," the captain added with a rather wicked smile, which spoiled the soothing effect of his previous words altogether and caused Marianne to nearly lose her composure.

"I am very grateful to you for giving me time to escape the library earlier," Marianne said stiffly, feeling the blood racing to her face. "And for coming to my rescue just now. Although really, you have saved yourself a great deal more discomfort than I, for you would be forced to listen to my singularly unskilled performance on the pianoforte while maintaining the pretense of a polite smile."

"In that case, I am most certainly glad, for I am hopeless at maintaining any sort of pretense, I fear," he admitted, looking utterly unapologetic.

Marianne had no reply to offer, for she herself felt exactly the same way, but had no desire to appear as though she were attempting to align herself with him any further than she already had. After smiling at her rather quizzically for another moment, Captain Larkin offered her a bow that was perfectly polite, and yet, the gesture left her heart racing, yet again. She told herself that she was altogether quite relieved when he took his leave and went to speak to her father. She was afforded a few minutes respite to gather her wits before there was yet another entertainment catastrophe for her to avert.

CHAPTER 4

When the last of the guests had – *finally* - said their farewells, Marianne felt as though she would like nothing more in the world than to collapse into a useless heap in the middle of the disheveled drawing room. Of course, she did not act on the impulse, primarily because her father and sister were still present. Nor did she care for the idea of admitting to either of them just how taxing the evening had been. No matter what Captain Larkin might have thought, a great many aggravatingly trivial details *had* gone wrong, and other guests, not accustomed to a rough military lifestyle, had certainly noticed.

While none of the problems seemed to be earth-shattering, Marianne knew for a fact that if they reached Arabella's ears, she would certainly feel the need to resume her mantle, at least in part, as lady of the Sedgewick estate. Not for anything would Marianne want her sister to feel guilty for focusing on establishing her own household with her new husband, so in that sense those problems *were* earth-shattering.

And really, the fact that no less than three members of the household staff were currently in tears certainly indicated some sort of organizational crisis. Before she could summon a sufficient amount of willpower to hunt down the housekeeper and dive into that foray, though, Marianne was distracted by her father speaking to her.

"Thank you, my dear, for being such a charming hostess for my guests this evening," Lord Sedgewick said kindly, as he and his daughters sipped chocolate before retiring for the evening.

"I hope I can do better in the future," Marianne said ruefully, and her father did not pretend to be ignorant about the various mishaps of the evening.

She would not have wanted him to, even had such pretense occurred to the earl, for it would have marred her delight that he had even thought to thank her. For a great many years, following the death of his wife, her father had retreated into a self-indulgent, albeit understandable, state of detachment. This had left Arabella and Marianne largely on their own, at sea as to how to cope without their mother, struggling to take care of little Daphne. After a time, it had seemed to be simply the natural way of things, with no one in the Sedgewick family questioning their roles.

She knew her father had gradually become aware of what a burden Arabella in particular had borne, and

Marianne had secretly hoped that he would perhaps not lean so heavily upon her in turn.

"I have the utmost confidence that you will, some skills are only acquired through experience, you know. A theoretical understanding does not always replace a practical one. But if it encourages you, I will tell you that the first dinner party your mother presided over was an unmitigated disaster."

"I can hardly imagine that," Marianne laughed despite her fatigue. She was greatly surprised that her father had voluntarily brought up a memory of the late Lady Sedgewick, as his grief had always been too sharp to allow for casual reminiscences, and Marianne wanted to make sure that she did nothing to discourage him from telling the rest of his story. She turned her full attention to her father.

"Oh, you may well believe it. All the details escape me now, which is hardly a surprise, considering the fact that your mother insisted I swear an oath to never mention them again, but if memory serves, the troubles began with a sadly overdone roast. I believe there was something the matter with the cook," he said thoughtfully. "I don't remember the particulars. And then, several guests were seated near one another who had, unbeknownst to us, a bitter feud with one another. By the end of the evening, one lady had been slapped by another, several people were in tears, more than a few old scandals had been dragged into the light, resulting in no less than two broken engagements. And a breach of promise lawsuit, unless I am confusing that with another occasion."

"What a perfect comedy of errors," exclaimed Daphne delightedly, drawing nearer. "Although I suppose it did not seem very humorous at the time."

"Certainly, it did not," agreed the earl with an emphatic nod of his dignified grey head. "Your mother cried herself to sleep for nearly a fortnight and swore she would never venture beyond our walls again. Such calamities require time before they can be regarded with anything like an accurate perspective."

"In that light, then, I hope I will have a few days' time, at least, before I must play hostess again," Marianne said fervently. "And as I seem to have offended Mr. Baxley quite deeply and horrified his proper sensibilities with my unladylike intellectual interests, he may spread the word so thoroughly that you find yourself decidedly short of friends and acquaintances to entertain."

"Baxley," Lord Sedgewick snorted with such contempt that Marianne and Daphne both giggled involuntarily. "I would scarcely have termed him a friend or an acquaintance, and I certainly shall not after hearing that he is offended by the idea of a lady who is more intelligent than himself. How he supposes he will find a suitable lady who is *not* more intelligent than himself is a mystery to me, however. The man seems to be an utter fool."

Marianne shook her head and chuckled, feeling a great deal of love for her father at that moment. "Perhaps, Papa," she said, "But he is a fool with an opinion that is shared by a great many of his peers." Marianne ignored the slight pang that she always felt when she thought too closely about the fact that her intellect was likely to ward off any serious suitors. She did not mind so much since she had little patience and less interest in such shallow-minded gentlemen anyhow. But the thought of being shut out from any chance of true companionship and love for her entire life *did* hurt.

"Not all of them, though," piped up Daphne brightly. The child seemed to be more alert and cheerful at that late hour than she had at the beginning of the dinner party, Marianne observed with some amusement. "I overheard Captain Larkin telling his brother as they were leaving that there was nothing so appealing as a lady who did not pretend silliness for the sake of pampering anyone's fragile vanity. I'm sure he was speaking of Baxley."

"And me," Marianne added, coloring slightly.

"You ought not to be eavesdropping on our guests, Daphne," the earl pointed out, but not so sternly as he would have if the girl had not been reinforcing his own point.

"I didn't need to eavesdrop," Daphne countered calmly. "Captain Larkin was speaking *very* loudly and distinctly. I rather thought that he meant for someone besides his brother to overhear him. Not me, I mean, someone with fragile vanity."

"That certainly rules you out then," Marianne murmured, a little absent-mindedly. She could easily guess who the captain had aimed his comment toward, even had she not happened to see that he left at the same time as Mr. Baxley. "There is nothing fragile about your vanity."

"Why should there be?" wondered Daphne in all sincerity. "And anyway, Captain Larkin is quite right. *And* quite handsome."

"Never mind telling us about how handsome a gentleman is," said the earl with a cough. "It is hardly a matter of importance."

"It would be important enough if a gentleman were ugly, I should think," Daphne retorted unrepentantly. "Or bald," she added with an entirely unladylike eyeroll, and Marianne's thoughts went to Mr. Baxley.

She shook her head to rid herself of the thought, and another face appeared before her mind's eye. Captain Larkin.

The night had indeed been one she would not wish to relive, except for the moment when Captain Larkin held her gloved hand and kissed it. For some reason, that singular moment stuck out in her mind with shining clarity, as if it were of some import.

"What is it?" Daphne asked.

"Nothing," she answered. "I am only tired."

Marianne was relieved when the conversation was allowed to end there. In addition to feeling horribly tired, she was beginning to grow unreasonably irritable, she realized. Why should she mind if Daphne said Captain Larkin was handsome? It was an empirical fact, after all.

She was glad to finally retire to the solitude of her bedchamber, but sleep escaped her even once she was settled cozily in her bed. There seemed to be far too many thoughts chasing one another through her mind, and she disliked the sensation of being unable to order or organize them properly. Her surprise and pleasure that her father had shared a memory of her mother was mingled with concern and annoyance at Mr. Baxley's unsurprising attitudes.

Beneath it all, however, she was thinking of Captain Larkin and the way he had covered for her so smoothly when she had needed time to escape the library, and the way he had looked ready to do battle with Mr. Baxley for insulting her. He had looked ridiculously handsome, really, she decided. There was something undeniably appealing about a gentleman who was strong and capable of action - violence, even, Marianne supposed, for he *had* been in battles, after all.

The thought made her blood rise most inexplicably, and she pressed her hands to her warm cheeks. She seemed to feel exceedingly warm all over. The feeling was most disconcerting. Surely, it had nothing to do with the captain. She attempted to examine the matter in a detached and logical fashion, but in vain. Especially when she recalled the fact that although Captain Larkin had seemed instantly ready to rise to her defense, he had also subsided with no apparent wounds to his ego when she had spoken for herself. *That* was far more appealing – and certainly a rarity, she thought. It was hardly any wonder that her heart raced and her face flushed whenever she encountered such a man.

"I am really just as bad as Daphne, or Ellen when she was younger, giggling and acting giddy over a gentleman's appearance," murmured Marianne, amused at herself as she pulled the coverlet over her limbs, blew out the candle and closed her eyes.

Unbidden, a long-discarded memory flooded her mind. She must have been very young, for her mother had still been with them, and they had been visiting some friends in a different part of the country. It had been summertime, and there had been the most fascinating boy there. He could not have really been too many years older than Marianne, she realized, but at the time he had seemed so tall and strong that she had been in awe of him as nearly a grown man.

He had fought another boy for her - an odious, overly plump boy who had pinched and taunted her, and then, unforgivably, snatched a book from her hands and flung it into the mud for no other reason than because he could.

Marianne could not recall the boys with any clarity, but she could remember vividly that she had been outraged and infuriated to the point of tears, and she recalled the book. It had been Ovid's *Metamorphosis*, her first volume. She remembered because she had been both captivated and overwhelmed with the text. She struggled to read the story of Daphne evading Apollo. It was especially riveting as she had a younger sister named Daphne, and she also remembered that she had tried in vain, to explain the story to her younger sister. That, at least, had not changed, she thought with a wry smile.

Daphne was always more interested in action than in reading.

In any case, who would do such a thing as throw a book into the mud? Thinking of the incident now brought on a whole new wave of anger at the unknown boy. She only remembered in the fuzzy, hazy way one did when on the verge of dreamland. She had been vindicated almost at once, but of course, the book was ruined. And now she was almost certain that the tall, wonderful youth who had pummeled the pudgy bully until that unfortunate creature ran away shrieking for his mother – *surely* that had been none other than young Andrew Larkin. She stared for a moment into the darkness.

That charming, slightly crooked grin, and the lightning-fast change from apparent indolence to action. There was no mistaking it. Marianne was suddenly confident. It was certainly probable that their families had been at the same place at the same time. She knew that Mrs. Millworth was a great friend of Lady Larkin, and had likewise been quite close with Marianne's mother.

Marianne stirred against her pillows with a rather dramatic groan. The connection would certainly explain her unusual reaction to Captain Larkin' presence. It did very little to reassure her. For anytime she had been drawn into a girlish discussion with Arabella and Ellen about the sort of gentleman they hoped to marry one day, she had always described *him*. At some point, she had forgotten the actual incident, or that her mythical ideal husband was a real person, but their brief interaction had continued to form the basis of her ideals.

And Captain Larkin was remaining in the neighborhood for some undetermined length of time, waiting for the wedding of his brother to Ellen, an event which would surely result in a great many further meetings. For the life of her, Marianne could not determine if this thought was exciting or mortifying.

CHAPTER 5

Andrew Larkin flung himself restlessly onto one of the armchairs in his brother's study, forgetting until it was too late that all the furniture was even dustier than usual. Aside from the questionable habits of Doctor Larkin' former series of housekeepers, a flurry of renovations was taking place in his house all in preparation for the arrival of the future Mrs. Larkin. Roger had never paid much notice to his environment or creature comforts previously, but having secured the heart of the lady of his dreams had changed the doctor's priorities drastically. Entire rooms were being added on to the old cottage, to say nothing of the general tearing apart and refreshing of the existing sections.

The study remained untouched so far, at least. Although Andrew had no doubt that the cluttered room would receive a similar treatment soon enough, but the disturbance and construction elsewhere had certainly deposited an amazing level of dust in even this sanctuary of his brother's.

Coughing and waving an arm to clear the air, Andrew took the assault on his lungs as philosophically as he could, reminding himself that he had certainly endured far worse, and would undoubtedly endure worse in the future as well.

"Sorry about that," Roger said apologetically, looking up from his current medical journal with an owlish air of surprise. Doubtless he had forgotten that he had a houseguest in the first place, Andrew guessed without rancor. It was impossible to resent his older brother's recent abstraction, particularly remembering how close the doctor had come to death not so long before.

"I do not mind for my own sake, so much, but surely this dust is not helpful for your patients?"

"Ah, well, I never offer the cushioned chairs to them," Roger pointed out, gesturing to the safer wooden chairs that *were* more prominently placed. "And I call on my patients whenever it is remotely possible, so few of them have occasion to visit here."

"I suppose all of this renovation will be completed before too much longer, at any rate," Andrew observed, but his brother shook his head sadly.

Andrew arched an eyebrow at Roger. "No?" he asked.

"I've just had another letter from our mother, I'm afraid," Roger said. "She informs me that even with the additional rooms and everything else, this is no fit place to present to a bride. She is sending some architect to take matter in hand. I believe the man's prestigious reputation is far greater than the home of a country doctor merits, but the poor gentleman is undoubtedly too intimidated to tell Mother that."

"He would be a singularly brave architect if he were otherwise than intimidated by Lady Larkin," the captain reflected, his own attitude of resignation matching his brother's almost perfectly. They adored their mother, without question, but no one of their acquaintance, or they themselves could deny that Lady Larkin was a force to be reckoned with.

"In her letter, Mother says the man will arrive here the day after tomorrow. Therefore, I believe we can safely assume he is an ordinary mortal," laughed the doctor. "But what is all this?"

Andrew was confused for a moment, before recalling he had entered the study clutching a handful of papers, which his brother had just now noticed with a nod of his head.

"Oh, these?" he gave the papers a look of deep disgust. "A great deal of annoyance, as it happens. I am in a position to have some say in my next assignment, particularly as I will be kicking my heels here until your wedding day. There are several options, which have been sent for my consideration. However, they are the dullest, most unappealing lot of prospects that could be found. Mother has had her hand in this just as surely as she selected your architect."

"Meaning that you are rather less likely to suffer from a loss of life or limb on any of these assignments, I suppose?" asked Roger mildly, familiar with the contention between their mother and his action-oriented brother.

"On the contrary, I would be in very grave danger," Andrew retorted, flinging the papers to the floor contemptuously. "I have no doubt that I should go utterly mad from boredom with any of these assignments, which of course will drive me to commit no end of reckless mischief. Surely, as a respected physician, you could write to Mother and assure her, that the medical profession has determined it is more than possible for a man to die of boredom? This is all your fault, after all."

"*My* fault?" the doctor looked torn between amused sympathy and bewilderment. "Whatever did I do?"

"What did you do?" Andrew said with exasperation. "Nothing more than follow the trail of a desperate, murderous lunatic, nearly managing to become the next victim. I have it on good authority that Mother was *highly* upset at your close call, especially considering she had made up her mind that you were safely tucked away in a sleepy little country village and unlikely to encounter much danger. She had practically made her peace with the risks I take in my profession, but your little adventure here has made her reassess everything."

"It was terribly thoughtless of me, almost dying like that," returned Roger dryly. "I can assure Mother that I will never again accept a cup of tea from a criminally insane person, if you think it will help matters at all."

"It is not a laughing matter," Andrew said, struggling to keep his scowl in place nonetheless. "Somehow or the other, our mother has the ear of absolutely everyone of consequence, and they are all quite loathe to refuse her demands. If Miss Millworth had not managed to save your wretched hide in the nick of time, Mother would undoubtedly have ordered the two of us as well as John and Percy home to be packed in cotton wool.

"And what of Charlie?" asked Roger. "After all he is the baby of the family."

"Oh, I'm sure Mother thinks him safe at his school."

"She obviously has no notion of the shenanigans that go on at a boarding school," Roger muttered.

"And Charlie will thank us to keep it that way," Andrew added.

"Yes, well, if Mother was so incensed, I would suppose that the rest of you are all indebted to Miss Millworth and myself," Roger pointed out archly. "Rather than blaming me, you ought to be thanking me, I should think."

Andrew paused for a moment, then gave in to the impulse to laugh. "Trust you to turn it all around on me. But truly, Roger, between being ordered to stay here until John can return from his business abroad and having only the prospect of astonishingly dull commissions awaiting me after your wedding, I have no idea what to do with myself."

"You always have been a creature of action," his brother concurred in an understanding tone."

The two brothers had almost perfectly dissimilar personalities, yet they had generally been sympathetic to one another's plights.

As the younger sons of a large and wealthy family, neither stood to inherit their father's title or fortune. They were, however, well provided for without the obligations and responsibilities that their brother John was prepared to bear. With the support of affectionate parents who nevertheless encouraged their sons to be industrious rather than idle. All of the siblings had been granted the liberty of pursuing callings that they truly loved.

Neither Roger nor Andrew was ignorant of their privilege, and although their mother's over-zealous attention could grate at times, all of the young gentlemen appreciated their family wholeheartedly.

"And there is little action to be had here, you must admit. You and your fiancée vanquished a deranged poisoner, and the new Lady Willingham defeated a fraudulent kidnapper. I daresay those two events used all the drama allotted to this sleepy little village for the next fifty years, perhaps more."

"I certainly hope that is true. For the life of me, I will never understand what is so appealing about such escapades. And *you* must admit that those things were fairly tame compared to your regular line of work."

Doctor Larkin raised a speculative eyebrow. "But surely you will find something of sufficient interest to occupy your time here."

"If I don't find something soon, I may very well go haring off after John and drag him home by the collar. You wouldn't object to a sooner wedding date, I suppose?" It was Andrew's turn to eye his brother with an arched eyebrow, as well as a rakish grin.

"By no means," Roger agreed so fervently that Andrew felt a sudden and unexpected pang of jealousy.

Unbidden, the image of Lady Marianne's face flashed into his mind. He was always caught off guard by her beauty, and always needed a few moments to acclimate himself to the excellence of her countenance. The more he looked upon her face, the stronger his belief that she was a Greek goddess, perfectly fashioned out of serene marble, with hues of gold and rose. The contrast of her delicate looks with her rapier sharp, logical mind was quickly becoming a fascination to observe, to touch and perhaps to have, and yet how could he ever hope to have such a creature?

She was perhaps the only woman who really tested his resolution to remain unmarried. Andrew had to admit that fact to himself if he were being strictly honest, and a captain in service to the crown, he never permitted himself the folly of self-deception.

That was the reason that he knew unequivocally that he could never be contented with a settled, stationary existence, and it would be monstrously unfair to take a wife and then leave her to live a solitary life for the majority of the time. He had seen firsthand the struggles married officers on active duty faced, and the misery that so many of their wives endured, but to have such a woman as Lady Marianne as his own…. He shook off the thought as unrealistic. She would not marry a mere soldier, and he would not take her from the pedestal on which she belonged.

"What is it like, Roger? Being in love?" he asked his brother, without really intending to speak at all. He could hear a note of wistfulness in his own voice, which surprised him even more than the fact he'd asked the question in the first place. Clearly staying in a drowsy village for so long was having some sort of weakening effect on his character.

"Until recently, I should have said that it was the worst and most unendurable misery of my entire life," his brother replied candidly. "Unrequited love is the most dire of circumstance, but things have certainly improved beyond my wildest hopes and dreams since Miss Millworth has told me she loves me."

His brother positively shone with happiness.

"Humph," said the captain. How terrifying, he thought, to wait upon the whims of a woman. He would not do so, no matter how intriguing he found Lady Marianne.

Perhaps it would be best if he avoided her altogether. Yes, he thought. That would be best for both of them.

CHAPTER 6

Lady Marianne could have sworn she felt the weight of the entire household lift from her shoulders as she slipped out a side door and made her way down the chilly lane to pay a call on the Millworth family. It had been an undeniably trying day, and she was fully aware of the fact that it was not quite three o'clock in the afternoon and therefore the day still had innumerable opportunities to present her with more difficulties.

It was really too cold for even the short walk, but Marianne was certain she would have deferred her outing for nothing short of an Arctic blizzard. Besides, the path was so familiar, her walk seemed to take no time at all. Rather, it was not quite enough time for the wintry air to blow away all the minor irritations that had been plaguing her.

"Oh, Marianne. I was just telling Mama that I hoped we would see you today, and here you are," exclaimed Ellen delightedly as soon as Marianne shed her pelisse and was shown into the comfortable sitting room.

"You may well wish otherwise," Marianne replied, only half in jest. "Trouble and aggravation seem to be following me about today, as if I were a perfect magnet for them."

"Why? What is wrong?"

"Oh, nothing to speak of, really," Marianne admitted, allowing herself to be led to a cozy armchair near the fire. She had been right to flee to the cheer of the Millworth estate, she decided, since it was all but impossible to remain cross in the company of Ellen and Mrs. Millworth. "Daphne has tormented her music instructor to the point of actual tears, and she feels equally exasperated with him, I believe. Not that I can understand half of what they are quarreling about. Father received a letter that required him to leave at once for London to deal with some minor business matter, and he was none too pleased about *that*. I seem to have offended Mrs. Gardener quite dreadfully at the dinner party the other evening, and for the life of me I cannot imagine how. I have been racking my brain all morning in an effort to determine what I must apologize for."

"Oh, dear," Mrs. Millworth began, sympathetically, but Marianne found that she could not quite manage to stem her flow of grievances once she had opened the floodgates.

"*And* there is some mysterious and very grim battle taking place among the household staff, the origins of which apparently date back as far as twenty years, not that any of them will enlighten me. Arabella's leaving seems to have made them draw their lines in the sand more stubbornly than ever. Two parlor maids took their leave of our employment today, and everyone else has seen fit to go about their duties with a great deal of ill grace and harsh looks. And how on earth I am going to sort it all out without asking Arabella and worrying her, I cannot begin to fathom. There is no particular reason for everything to go wrong all at once, but it *has* been such a heap of problems that I am half inclined to wonder if there is something to be said for all of those superstitions about full moons."

"Poor lamb," said Mrs. Millworth in her soothing, motherly voice, although there was a distinct note of laughter in her tone. "Some days do just seem filled with more than their share of trouble, don't they? But no day lasts forever, luckily enough. And even more luckily it will be quite easy for you to make amends with Mrs. Gardener, at least. She was here the other day, airing her grievances, so I can shed some light on that problem. Mrs. Gardner was upset because you had seated her across from Sir Allen at dinner, and the woman thought you must have done it on purpose to slight her because she has been at odds with his entire family for a dozen years. She has said repeatedly that she could not bear the sight of their faces. In Mrs. Gardner's mind, the only reason someone would seat her across from any of the Allens is to tacitly discourage her from accepting any future invitations. But I imagine that if you plead ignorance, she will forgive you readily enough. She does know that Arabella usually took care of such things in the past."

"Good heavens, I can plead my ignorance with complete sincerity. I never heard of such a quarrel existing between them," Marianne said in mortification at her mistake.

"Well, you have never paid very much mind to local gossip, so I have no doubt that Mrs. Gardener will believe you," Ellen interjected helpfully. "Perhaps if you looked at it as a sort of study in history or some type of philosophy, you might have an easier time familiarizing yourself with it all."

"Do you know, I believe you are right," Marianne laughed after taking a moment to consider the suggestion. "Although I am beginning to suspect that it may all be more complicated and confusing than the entirety of our national history."

"Still, if you can untangle all of *those* dates and feuds and bloodlines, this shouldn't prove to be so much of a challenge."

"I am certainly glad I came to call today, and happier still to have such sympathetic listeners," said Marianne, feeling all of her petty woes slip like magic back into a proper perspective. "But that cannot possibly be the reason that you wanted to see me, Ellen. What was it that you needed?"

"Oh, only to find out if you have had any word from Lady Willingham regarding her return to the village," Ellen admitted with an impish smile for her sister

Arabella's new title. "I am missing her more than I would one of my own limbs, especially with my mind so filled with wedding preparations. I am very much missing my best friend.

"As a matter of fact, I had a letter from her only just yesterday. We may look for her arrival as soon as the day after tomorrow."

"Surely you aren't fretting about that as well?" Mrs. Millworth asked, making Marianne wince.

"I had thought I was doing a better job of concealing that," she confessed ruefully. "I am either a very poor actress or you are entirely too perceptive."

"Perhaps it is a little of both," suggested Mrs. Millworth mildly. "But I should imagine that whatever your concern is, it will prove unfounded. There never were two sisters who understood each other half so well as Arabella and yourself."

"Yes, and that is a great portion of my concern. It will not be a simple matter to keep my foolish mistakes and impatience concealed from Arabella when she is home. She has spared the rest of us so much trouble, far more than her fair share, you know, and I am afraid she will have a harder time than she thinks when it comes to letting me muddle along until I am at least reasonably competent. And worse, really, I fear I will selfishly revert to old habits and accidentally rely upon her too much when she ought to be thinking only of her new home and husband."

Marianne concluded her confession with a dispirited little sigh, for she could imagine far too easily how great the temptation to slip back into those familiar roles. Mrs. Millworth placed a comforting hand on hers, and gave her a smile.

"I should think that being aware of such a likelihood will be more than half of the battle, my dear. You have a good heart and you love your sister, and she loves you. The rest will all follow."

"I hope so," Marianne said, fighting a sudden and irrational rush of tears. Why the reassuring words and gesture touched her so suddenly she could not have said, but she felt a wave of gratitude towards the motherly presence of Mrs. Millworth.

Ellen tactfully turned the conversation towards lighter topics, sensing, perhaps, that Marianne did not wish to give way to crying in their presence. The three women passed a pleasant half hour simply enjoying one another's company, and Marianne was just beginning to feel that perhaps the ill-favored day was taking a turn for the better, when a rumble of masculine voices in the foyer told her that perhaps she had relaxed her guard too soon.

"Oh, the men must be back from shooting." cried Ellen happily, her cheeks flushing prettily, which confirmed Marianne's suspicion that Doctor Larkin was included in the hunting party.

"I did not realize that the doctor enjoyed that sort of sport," Marianne teased, attempting to make her tone light and jesting. In truth, she was feeling decidedly nettled, for she was certain that where one Larkin brother was the other was certain to be, as well. She had still been unable to decide how she felt about her recent realization that Captain Larkin was her childhood daydream, and had therefore been making a valiant attempt to shut out any thought of him at all.

"Well, it is certainly not his first choice of a pastime, but between his sense of obligation to keep his brother occupied and entertained, and his desire to stay in my father's good graces, he is resigned to make the best of it," Ellen laughed.

The gentlemen stomped into the sitting room presently, and Marianne saw that she had been correct in assuming that Captain Larkin would be included in the hunting party. The gentlemen were laughing and joking with one another in loud voices and comradery. They brought with them the fresh odor of the outdoors and the distinctive scent of horses and leather. It was not an altogether unpleasant smell, and combined with the sight of the captain himself, it was quite heady. Marianne did her best to keep her expression neutral and pleasant as her heart gave the silly leap that she was beginning to associate with the sight of him. She glanced up at him through her long lashes, her own cheeks rosy with anticipation of the conversation to come. She could not stop the small smile that had spread across her face.

Mr. Millworth looked well pleased with both his afternoon and his company, and his future son-in-law seemed to have enjoyed the sporting well enough. Although, Marianne suspected he had deliberately aimed away from any pheasants that he had been unfortunate enough to sight. As for the captain, he appeared to be energized and in good spirits, doubtless having enjoyed the exercise and sport as being more akin to his natural element.

Marianne was suddenly aware of the pairing of the assembled party for Mr. and Mrs. Millworth automatically turned their attention to one another, as did Doctor Larkin and Ellen. It was only natural, of course, but it had the unfortunate consequence of throwing Marianne and Captain Larkin together by default.

She could not read the man's expression very well, particularly since she was doing her best to keep from looking directly into his eyes. She was certain he would be able to read something of her confused emotions if she did so, and the conviction that she would inevitably make a fool of herself one way or another was practically paralyzing. If only she had cut short her visit by a few minutes.

Before Marianne could decently make her escape, but sadly, not before she had exhausted her limited reserves of uninteresting and safe topics of conversation, the Millworth's butler appeared in the doorway of the sitting room. He was accompanied by a man that Marianne thought she recognized as the regular driver for the express, who was looking awkward and apologetic, and a small, shabbily dressed girl.

"Begging your pardons," the driver said, clearly uncomfortable, crumpling his hat in his hand. "I called first at Doctor Larkin's home but was told there that the gentlemen were likely to be here all afternoon. I would have waited, but I have to get on with my route, you know. I'm terribly late as it is."

"Certainly, that was quite right," Doctor Larkin said encouragingly. "Do you require medical attention?"

"Ah, no sir. I was told that Captain Larkin was staying there or here. I mean with you, doctor. Would that be you, sir?" the driver addressed the captain, more apologetically than ever.

"Yes, I am Captain Larkin," he replied, and Marianne thought the captain was every bit as mystified at the turn of events as everyone else in the room.

"Oh, that's a relief, sir, and I don't mind saying so. I'm to deliver this young lady to your keeping," the man said gesturing at a bedraggled child who looked to be about ten and jamming his hat back on his head. "She has a letter as will explain it all, she tells me." Before anyone could say a word, the man bowed and hurried out of the room, leaving the little girl staring rather blankly at the astonished party.

CHAPTER 7

Captain Larkin was undoubtedly a man of action, both by profession and personality, but that characteristic did not appear to extend to the delivery of mysterious children to his care. In fact, Marianne noted during the somewhat electrified silence that reigned over the sitting room, the man was actually *more* paralyzed by the unexpected situation than his civilian counterparts.

It was Mrs. Millworth who recovered her wits first, giving herself a little shake and then rising to cross the room and smile reassuringly at the little girl.

"Hello, dear, why don't you come and sit beside the fire. I expect you must be quite chilled to the bone, traveling in this cold weather. Let's get you warmed up, perhaps you would care for some tea?"

"Broth would be better," Doctor Larkin interposed, evidently having given the child a visual examination.

Marianne did not know what his exact medical opinion might have been, but she could see for herself that the child's pallor, emphasized by dark circles below her eyes and the decidedly blue cast of her fingertips, seemed to recommend careful nourishment and rest.

"Broth, certainly," nodded Mrs. Millworth in the direction of the butler, who departed immediately. She drew the child gently to an armchair near the fire, but the little girl seemed to balk at actually taking a seat.

"I have a letter for Captain Andrew Larkin. I must give it to him right away," she said in a weary but determined voice, her eyes fixed upon the captain's face.

This seemed to jolt him out of his astonished trance. "You are Lieutenant Henry Southampton's child, are you not? You look a great deal like your father."

"Yes, sir. I am Elizabeth Southampton," she replied, opening her small reticule and pulling a crumpled paper from its environs. She stood holding out the worn letter to the captain with an unreadable expression on her pale little face. Her hand was visibly trembling.

Marianne thought that everyone else in the room seemed to let out a furtive breath of relief at this exchange, and she realized she had not been the only one to wonder if Captain Larkin had been about to reveal a secret marriage and family. She felt a flush of guilt at her assumption and could see from the uneasy way her companions were shifting about that she was not alone in that sensation either.

"But where *is* your father?" Captain Larkin was asking, taking the letter from the little girl's hand but not looking at it. "However, did you come here all the way from Dover by yourself?"

"My father died, not quite a fortnight ago."

Mrs. Millworth gasped at the bleak news.

"It was very sudden," she said her voice devoid of emotion. "And he left me explicit instructions to come here and find you, sir, or if you were not here to find your brother so that he might send word to you," answered Elizabeth Southampton in the weary voice of someone reciting a tiresome lesson. Marianne saw that the little girl was suppressing tears with a great deal of effort. The child's lips trembled a bit as she spoke, and her fingers clenched tightly together to stop their shaking.

"Was there no one to accompany you, dear? That is a terribly long journey for a child to embark upon alone. I am amazed you were allowed to leave home by yourself," Mr. Millworth wondered.

"No, ma'am. My mother died when I was born, and Father said that we have no other family. We used to have a little cottage very near the sea, and I stayed there with our housekeeper, Mrs. Gilford. She looked after me whenever Father had to be away. But Mrs. Gilford had to leave when the cottage was sold a while ago. Father and I have been staying in rooms at the inn. I could not keep staying there after he died. The man in charge of the inn said Father had owed him a great deal of money. He took most of the money that he found in my father's things, to cover the bill, but he left me enough to pay for a ride here on the express coach."

This burst of communication proved to be more than the poor child could manage while keeping her tears at bay. She concluded her speech by burying her face in her hands, her body racked with her muffled, heartbroken sobs.

"Oh, there, poor thing, you need not try to talk," soothed Mrs. Millworth, gathering Elizabeth into her arms comfortingly while simultaneously sending her husband an exasperated look. "No one will interrogate you any further. I am sure your father's letter explains everything."

"I think perhaps Miss Southampton ought to lie down, if we might presume upon your hospitality," Doctor Larkin suggested, and his future mother-in-law nodded her approval of the idea.

When Mrs. Millworth had bustled the child competently out of the sitting room, all attention returned to Captain Larkin, who seemed to be rooted to the spot, transfixed by the letter in his hands.

"What does it say?" prompted his brother.

The captain shook himself visibly and folded the letter, putting it away in his vest pocket with a blank expression that arrowed straight to Marianne's heart. He seemed to be stowing away his feelings along with the worn paper. "Essentially the same things that the child herself has just related. His physician told him that he was growing very close to death and, having no family or closer connections, Southampton felt his daughter's future had better be entrusted to myself. In his letter, he apologized several times over, feeling he was unfairly burdening me and perhaps presuming too much on our friendship. But he expressed that no amount of delicate feelings could overpower a parent's desire to give their child the best possible prospects."

"That is certainly true," Mr. Millworth agreed, evidently approving of the unknown soldier's sentiment. "I suppose you knew the lieutenant quite well, for him to consider your worthy of such a trust and willing to shoulder such a responsibility?"

"Henry Southampton has been my brother in arms for a great many dangerous campaigns. I have counted him as my closest friend for quite some time. To receive word of his death so unexpectedly is among the worst shocks that I have ever known," replied Captain Larkin, and the raw grief in his eyes made Marianne blink her own eyes fiercely against sudden sympathetic tears. "One is prepared for such things, of course, in the heat of battle. I find it is another thing altogether to lose a comrade in this commonplace way. Henry seemed as hale and hearty as ever when we embarked on our leave, and yet his letter informs me that he was dying of consumption. Apparently, a sudden fever brought his symptoms to…this."

"There are forms of consumption, and indeed, other diseases altogether than are often mistaken for consumption that do not display the signs and symptoms one would expect until quite near the end," Doctor Larkin murmured, his tone and expression showing awareness that his brother was casting about guiltily, certain he had missed some important signs that might have saved his comrade's life. "It is quite likely that your lieutenant did not display any ill effects that you might have noticed until a fever settled in his lungs a fortnight or so before his death."

"He was ever the bravest and most unselfish man. Even in this letter he speaks of no concern for himself, no fear for his impending death, only concern for his daughter."

Captain Larkin accepted a glass of the port that Mr. Millworth had been silently been handing around, and raised it in a toast to his fallen friend. Marianne felt about blindly for her handkerchief, acknowledging to herself that blinking away her tears was ineffectual. The moment seemed to hum with a poignancy that made her think of every ancient tale of fallen heroes she had ever read, coloring those accounts with fresh emotion.

PART II

CHAPTER 8

Mrs. Millworth returned to the room, wiping away her own tears and taking her place beside her husband. "That poor little lamb is fast asleep already," she announced once the respectful silence seemed to naturally conclude. "And no wonder, traveling such a long way alone, while grieving for her father. I could barely get her into clean nightclothes and coax a bit of broth down her throat before her eyes closed. You must not think of disturbing her sleep, Andrew. I will not hear of the child being moved before tomorrow morning at the earliest."

"I think that would be for the best, if you are certain that you don't mind," the doctor agreed, with a sidelong glance at his brother. "There does not seem to be much wrong with the girl besides fatigue, although I daresay she looks a bit ill-nourished to my eye. I will give her a more thorough examination tomorrow, but I think we can safely say that she carries no contagion from her father's illness, at least."

"Such a thought had not even entered my mind," admitted Captain Larkin, looking rather shamefaced. "I apologize. I could have brought this contagion to you."

"Nonsense. The more important thing to be thinking of is what do you plan to do with the poor sweet child?" replied Mrs. Millworth briskly, raising her eyebrows at the captain expectantly.

"What do I plan to do with her? Why, I shall take care of her just as Henry requested, of course," he replied, looking startled at the very question. "What else would I do? Send her to an orphanage, or turn her out of the door to seek her fortune?"

"Of course, you wouldn't," Ellen put in gently, giving her future brother-in-law a warm smile. "But of course, that is precisely what *some* people might do, considering the circumstances."

"What circumstances could possibly justify such a reprehensible course of action?" Captain Larkin wondered, looking genuinely baffled by the idea.

"You are not a settled man with a permanent home, and you have no legal obligation to take on such a charge, after all," his brother pointed out in a mild tone, as if anticipating his brother's reaction to the explanation.

"My legal obligation can go hang," exclaimed the captain hotly. Then, recalling the gentle company, he said, "I beg your pardon, ladies, but I am far more concerned with my moral obligation in this matter, and my way seems perfectly clear. Henry Southampton saved my life more than once. I will never be able to repay my debt to him. Now he has left his only child in my care, and if I did not honor his request, I should never again be able to claim I had any honor whatsoever."

"Of course, you feel that way, dear," Mrs. Millworth said approvingly. "I should expect nothing less from you. I have no doubt whatsoever that you will manage the care of a child quite admirably. Are there any habitable rooms in your house just now, Roger?"

"Ah, yes, I believe so," replied the doctor after thinking for a moment. "Certainly, we can prepare something for her and have it ready by tomorrow afternoon."

"That's settled then. And you must see about finding some new clothes for the child, Andrew. The driver left her little bag, but it contained precious little."

"I expect we have some of Daphne's old things that might do, at least temporarily," Marianne heard herself saying, and Captain Larkin turned to give her a startled look, as if he had utterly forgotten her presence. "If that would be of any assistance?"

"I daresay it would, thank you, Lady Marianne," the captain replied gratefully. Marianne could only sigh to herself over the fact that his momentary notice warmed her heart.

"I will see about it, then," she murmured, deciding that it was high time for her to take her leave. Her visit to the

Millworth's home had certainly been a distraction from her own troubles, which seemed quite insignificant in contrast, but she could not claim that she felt any lighter in spirit at present. Her heart ached for the poor orphaned child.

"Whatever do you want with a bunch of my old dresses and things?" demanded Daphne with her characteristic blunt curiosity when she came upon Marianne sorting through her wardrobe later that evening.

"Captain Larkin discovered quite unexpectedly that he has a young ward," Marianne explained distractedly, frowning at the unsatisfactory contents of the wardrobe. "She appeared without any warning, and in possession of scarcely any worldly goods, so I thought to bundle up a few of your outgrown frocks for the poor thing."

"How perfectly thrilling." Daphne exclaimed with a delighted intake of breath at the very idea. "Just when Captain Larkin seems to be the most romantic figure imaginable, something like this happens to make him even *more* fascinating."

Marianne gritted her teeth at her younger sister's unfeeling comment or perhaps it was because the girl found the captain fascinating. In any case, the comment was completely unacceptable. "I doubt very much if Captain Larkin is particularly thrilled, considering he would not have guardianship of the child if not for the death of his dear friend," pointed out Marianne with asperity. "And one can hardly imagine that forlorn little girl cares much that her tragedy serves to make a stranger any number of degrees more or less fascinating."

"No, I suppose not," agreed Daphne, looking only slightly abashed. "It does seem like a very tragic situation, although you've not given me very much information. But if you think my old things would fit her then I suppose she must be somewhere around my own age?"

"I think she is a little younger than you are, dearest. At least she is a good deal shorter and slighter. I cannot imagine any of these things coming close to fitting poor Miss Southampton. Where are all the frocks that you've outgrown?"

"Why, Arabella always gives them to Mrs. Wilson for her daughters," Daphne said in a tone that implied surprise at Marianne's ignorance. Really, Marianne reflected, her ignorance regarding the inner workings of the household should hardly be a surprise to anyone, least of all her younger sister, but she supposed Daphne never paid much regard to anyone other than herself.

"That is right, of course. I wasn't thinking," she sighed, setting aside a pile of too-large dresses. "I suppose I will have to ask Philippa to take in a few of your current dresses, if you won't mind terribly, Daphne. Miss Southampton arrived with little more than the clothes on her back, and they were none too new themselves. I hardly think that either of the Larkin brothers are equal to the task of finding new clothes for her, as they were clearly taken by surprise by her arrival."

"Of course, I don't mind. Why, she can have every stitch I own for all I care," replied Daphne with perfect sincerity. "But I think there are some smaller things in the bottom drawer there, it was locked for the longest time because the key was lost, but I happened to find it just the other day."

"Where was it?"

"Oh, it was in a magpie's nest, along with any number of other little treasures," laughed the girl, rummaging around in her pockets before producing the small iron key.

Marianne briefly considered asking where the magpie's nest was, and how exactly Daphne had 'happened' upon it, but decided that she would much rather not actually know. Daphne could climb trees as nimbly as a squirrel, and no amount of scolding had impressed upon her sister the idea that such a pastime was not entirely ladylike.

Instead, she took the proffered key and unlocked the bottom drawer that her sister indicated.

"There, see." crowed Daphne triumphantly, seizing the contents of the drawer and holding them aloft. "All these dresses and things are from at least two years ago, and they are even the right season."

"I think they will do nicely," Marianne agreed, relieved that she would not have to admit failure after volunteering her help. If she were being perfectly honest, she could admit to herself that she was reluctant to appear any more foolish than she already had in front of Captain Larkin. The man undoubtedly thought her a foolish chit who was hardly worth his notice. That was probably why he had been so scarce lately. He didn't pay her a thought, and here she was enamored. Was that what she was, she wondered? Enamored? Surely not.

She shook out the articles of clothing, occasionally coming across a long-forgotten treasure of Daphne's, much to the girl's delight. She would have to ask one of the maids to wash and press everything before she could take the clothes to the Larkin's home, and she had learned just enough about running the household to know that an extra and unexpected request had the mysterious power to disrupt the entire staff, somehow. Really, it was like attempting to navigate the politics of a high-stakes court intrigue, all while blindfolded and ignorant of the various players, at that.

It was a token of just how much she did not wish to examine her confusing feelings regarding Captain Larkin that Marianne threw herself into the treacherous waters of staff dynamics instead. Between that daunting task, continuing to prepare for Arabella's return, and relating the full account of Elizabeth Southampton's appearance to Daphne and their father over dinner, Marianne succeeded in distracting her mind for the entire evening.

The accomplishment was so satisfying, she decided to prolong the inevitable even further, by taking a well-worn volume of Greek plays up to her bedchamber and losing herself in the pages until she grew too drowsy to keep her eyes open any longer.

CHAPTER 9

Marianne awoke refreshed and clear-headed the next morning. She had not, unfortunately, managed to come to any sort of resolution or conclusion in her sleep regarding her disorienting reaction to Captain Larkin. She thought perhaps there was no real resolution to be had. He was handsome and charming, but she had no doubt his plans left no space for romance. If they had, he surely would have pursued a companion long before the present, after all.

And undoubtedly such a companion would be a more conventional lady than herself, a thought that stung not a little. He had been very gallant in coming to her defense the other evening, but in reflecting upon the conversation Marianne concluded that his attitude was due more to chivalry and a sense of disdain for the weak-minded Mr. Baxley than an actual approval of her own intellect.

It was one thing to resign herself in an abstract sense to the idea that few gentlemen would care to wed someone so absorbed with 'indelicate' academic and intellectual pursuits. It was altogether different to think the literal personification of her ideal man would be disinterested in her for reasons she was utterly powerless to change. And she *was* powerless to change her essential nature, Marianne knew. She could perhaps mask or dilute it temporarily, but such deception would make no one happy, least of all herself.

Then again, she told herself objectively, she had no real notion if she really *did* have a romantic interest in Captain Larkin himself. In all reality she could not claim to know the man at all, only the ideal hero that he represented in her mind. She had witnessed firsthand the folly of falling in love with an idea of a man rather than the reality of him. Ellen Millworth's disastrous first engagement to a villainous fraud had shown her what catastrophic consequences such a situation could bring about. Marianne had no wish to make a similar mistake.

So, objectively, there was no resolution, because there was no problem, she concluded. They did not know one another, and even if they had the opportunity to become truly well-acquainted, they would be quite incompatible in all likelihood. There was nothing to be done, other than setting aside the irrational reaction she had to Captain Larkin's presence. Surely, that task would not prove to be so Herculean as it seemed.

Resolved, then, Marianne ruthlessly selected one of her least smart gowns for the day and told Philippa to not bother very much with styling her hair. She could hardly expect to overcome her foolish emotions while pampering her vanity, after all.

"Are you going to take those clothes to Captain Larkin's ward? I want to come with you, please Marianne," pleaded Daphne, predictably, as soon as she caught sight of Marianne taking up the basket of clothing.

"I imagined you would," Marianne laughed, nodding her assent and pausing at the door. She waited for Daphne to change her indoor slippers for boots and gather her own cloak.

"But I have an errand to run before I stop at the Larkin's home," Marianne cautioned. "Arabella and Lord Willingham are due to return this evening. I wish to stop by their house and make sure all is in readiness for them."

"I like that errand almost as much as the other," Daphne declared with enthusiasm. "And I can hardly wait to see Arabella and the Baron again, it seems as if they have been away for months and months. They must have so much to tell us."

"I daresay we will not see them until tomorrow morning at the earliest," Marianne felt compelled to caution her younger sister, as she saw signs of that enthusiasm burgeoning rather unrealistically. "They will be quite exhausted from traveling, you know, and may not arrive until quite late in the evening. And, you know, dearest, things will most likely have changed a great deal in their absence."

"Changed how?" Daphne wrestled with her wrap while effortlessly maintaining a brisk trot alongside Marianne.

Marianne kept her eyes forward as she made her way through the door, and all but ordered herself to refrain from blushing. "Oh, well, Arabella is a married woman now, you know."

"I don't really see how that would change her so much. Indeed, I don't believe that it will," said Daphne decidedly, casting a superior glance at Marianne as if to pity her for having such foolish, unfounded worries.

Marianne decided she had said more than enough on the subject and gave Daphne a smile. "You are right, I'm sure."

Their errand at Willowbend did not take long, for Lord Willingham's household staff had maintained the home beautifully in his absence. Marianne and Daphne left a little note and a bouquet of hothouse flowers, and some winter apples, but then Marianne had to admit that there was really nothing else for her to do, and she must stop putting off her real errand.

If Willowbend looked marvelously changed from the neglected old near-ruin it had been before Lord Willingham took ownership, Marianne reflected that the exact opposite might be said of Doctor Larkin's home. The charming old stone cottage had always seemed like a comforting haven, quite peaceful in spite of the haphazard ministrations of the doctor's former housekeeper. At present it was in a state of such visible disarray it was hardly recognizable. Marianne found herself stepping gingerly over disturbed paving stones and scattered bits of carpentry.

"What a mess," Daphne remarked with cheerful tactlessness as soon as she caught sight of Doctor Larkin's face. He smiled warmly, unoffended by the frank remark.

"It is a disaster, rather," he agreed. "Although my brother informs me it is not quite accurate to compare the place to a battle-scene. So, I must refrain from saying so, but between you and me, I can't say there seems to be much difference."

"If the battle you are waging is against your poor cottage, then perhaps you can make the comparison," suggested Daphne.

"Are you really able to host Miss Southampton here?" asked Marianne doubtfully. The noise and mess of the renovation seemed contrary to the peace and quiet the girl's plight surely demanded.

"Oh, certainly. The room we have made ready for her is the furthest away from all of this chaos, and the new housekeeper will be along in less than a fortnight. We shall muddle along well enough until then, I daresay," Dr. Larkin said reassuringly.

"Well, I would never dream of doubting your expert opinion," Marianne declared, although she felt far from convinced that the matter would be as simple as the doctor seemed to believe. "And I am certain that Miss Southampton will be glad enough to stay any place that isn't as dreadful- sounding as the inn she described yesterday, poor thing. I thought the innkeeper sounded like rather a villain, going through her dead father's things, and helping himself to his payment. He could easily have pocketed a great deal more than he was actually owed, with no one to say otherwise but a grief-stricken little girl."

"You did not mention that part of the story last night when you were telling Father and I all about Miss Southampton's appearance, Marianne," exclaimed Daphne with a decidedly fierce look. "How monstrous."

"Really, Elizabeth Southampton had quite a stroke of luck that she was at the mercy of that innkeeper and not a less honest man," Doctor Larkin averred, correctly interpreting Daphne's burst of outrage as the precursor to prompt vengeance if allowed to continue unchecked. "He may or may not have taken more than his fair share of the lieutenant's money to settle his account, but he did at least leave the child with enough to cover her fare on the express coach here. Such a thing is hardly heard of, but you may set your mind at ease, Lady Daphne, since I believe my brother has every intention of speaking with the innkeeper at his earliest convenience."

"Well then, that ought to suffice, for I am sure that Captain Larkin would not allow his ward to be cheated out of so much as a farthing of her inheritance," decided Daphne, whose confidence in the dashing captain gave Marianne an irrational flare of annoyance she had to quickly quench, only to have the feeling promptly reignited when Daphne asked, "Where *is* the captain, anyway?"

"He went to the Millworths to collect Miss Southampton, more than an hour ago, I believe. They ought to be back any time now."

"We should just leave these things and be on our way," Marianne said, ignoring Daphne's immediate protest. Marianne tried very hard to convince herself that if she could complete her errand and avoid seeing the captain, she would count herself fortunate indeed. "I am certain that it would be better for Miss Southampton to have a quiet introduction to her new home, and not be overwhelmed by an unnecessary surplus of new faces."

"No, here comes the carriage up the lane now," said Daphne with an unveiled expression of triumph. "We shall simply have to refrain from being overwhelming, I suppose."

CHAPTER 10

Marianne resigned herself as philosophically as she could to navigating the, hopefully brief, encounter, promising herself an afternoon spent in the lovely solitude of the library to gather her wits, once she returned home. She was frankly skeptical of Daphne's ability to refrain from being overwhelming, but she saw immediately that she had underestimated the power of her younger sister's kind and generous nature.

She greeted the timid girl with an infectious air of calm confidence and a smile that struck just the right balance between sympathetic and bracing. Miss Southampton responded to Daphne's friendly overtures with such obvious relief that Marianne realized how intimidated the girl must have been in the company of no one but unfamiliar adults. After only the briefest of introductions, Daphne blithely took charge of the situation and had commandeered the basket of clothes and asked permission to help Miss Southampton locate her new room.

The two girls left the three adults with scarcely a backwards glance, evidently the best of friends already. If Elizabeth Southampton had seemed frail and sickly the night before, her poor health was even more pronounced when contrasted directly with the vigorously healthy and golden Daphne. The girl was far too thin and pale, with heavy shadows beneath her eyes that a comfortable night's rest and a few good meals, courtesy of Mrs. Millworth's hospitality, had been powerless to erase.

"The poor little thing," murmured Marianne without thinking. "It really looks as though she has not had a proper meal in ages, doesn't it?"

She had addressed her question to Doctor Larkin, who nodded his agreement while also casting a wary glance at his brother. Marianne had not considered how the idea would affect the captain, but hazarding her own glance at the man she realized he was only barely suppressing a storm of unpleasant emotions.

"I beg your pardon, Captain Larkin, I did not mean to seem critical of your late friend, I assure you," she said quickly.

"You did not say anything that I wasn't already thinking, I assure you, Lady Marianne," the gentleman replied in a carefully controlled voice. "I had hoped my impression of the condition of Elizabeth's health was only due to her weariness and grief. But this morning, it was impossible to mistake her condition for anything else other than poor nourishment. I would be willing to wager my very soul on the fact that Harry Southampton loved his child more than anything else in the world. So, I can only imagine he took the worst of their meager circumstances upon himself. It is no small wonder his health deteriorated so rapidly; I suppose."

"Lack of adequate food and rest could certainly have accelerated the progression of the lieutenant's illness. Although, I cannot really make that claim without knowing the exact nature of that illness. It is just as likely that it would have made no difference at all in the rate of his decline. However, a lack of nourishment would certainly have made his last days a great deal less comfortable than they might otherwise have been," Captain Larkin's brother said with the gentle and steady tone that had soothed so many distraught and grieving relatives of his patients. "But just from the most cursory of visual examinations, I do not think that your new ward shows signs of prolonged deprivation. She is naturally slim and slight of form."

"Do you mean that it does not seem likely that they had been living in such poverty for an extended length of time?" asked Captain Larkin, looking slightly less distressed at the idea.

"Precisely. It looks to my eye as if perhaps the state of want has only been affecting the child for a matter of a few weeks, one or two months at most. Grief and her father's illness, and the travel here, certainly seems to have taken its toll, but she seems well-formed and not overly small for her age. It is clear that her intelligence and character have not been affected. While grief can have a lasting effect, I have no doubt that with proper care she will recover—eventually."

"That is good, of course," his brother said, still frowning. "But I cannot imagine for the life of me why Southampton would not have reached out to me sooner if he was in such dire straits. I cannot believe that it was a matter of pride, for he would have considered that but a small price to pay for to ensure the health and well-being of his beloved child. The entire situation is so utterly out of character for the man I knew. I can scarcely comprehend it at all, unless to think that I had somehow inadvertently given him the impression that I would be unwilling to come to his aid. I cannot imagine how or why he might have thought that, but it is really the only explanation I can deduce."

"Perhaps in his illness he was not thinking clearly?" Marianne could not refrain from suggesting. She felt her presence was terribly intrusive at the moment, and the captain's grief and confusion made her feel ashamed for having spent any length of time analyzing the foolish, fluttering rush of warmth he inspired, but she could not take her leave when Daphne was engaged with his ward.

In the face of his distress, she could see how mortifyingly pointless her resolve was to be strictly rational and unemotional. It was clear Captain Larkin's full attention was on his ward and nothing could be further from the man's mind than any sort of flirtation with her. Marianne determined more firmly than ever to retreat to her library at the earliest possible opportunity, not as a reward, however, but because she was so woefully ill-equipped to interact with others. It would be in the best interest of everyone if she kept to her books as much as possible. Until then, however, she would offer whatever consoling ideas she could.

"That is entirely likely, Lady Marianne," agreed Doctor Larkin, brisk and approving. Marianne did not know if her suggestion had as much merit as his manner implied, but she could tell that the doctor was first and foremost concerned with keeping his brother from sinking into a morass of guilt and self-recrimination that he might have somehow failed his friend. "It has often been observed that the thought processes of those suffering from serious illness are easily confused. Your friend must have known you would gladly give him assistance, Andrew, since the lieutenant ultimately entrusted his child to you. A final burst of clarity is also quite common in sufferers who are nearing their end. But truly, Andrew, there is nothing more likely than the idea that Lieutenant Southampton's thinking was clouded for a time by his illness, and he was simply unable to do anything more than survive each moment. You have seen similar behavior in men in battle, have you not?"

"I suppose that I have. To some extent I have even experienced such a phenomenon myself," admitted his younger brother somewhat begrudgingly. "But I daresay you would be perfectly capable of overemphasizing that possibility in order to spare me from some degree of my mental anguish."

"Oh, yes, I am quite capable of such a thing," Doctor Larkin said cheerfully. "I am your elder brother, after all, and my affection for you would leave me with no qualms whatsoever. You will kindly remember, though, that it was not *my* suggestion but Lady Marianne's. The lady possesses quite easily a keener intellect than anyone I know, including physicians with whom I have studied.

Besides that, you can hardly imagine that any sort of brotherly affection for you is coloring her words, now, can you?"

Marianne tried, and failed utterly, to conceal a blush at the doctor's final comment. She *had* made the suggestion out of affection for Captain Larkin, although admittedly she did not think her affection had any brotherly or sisterly qualities.

"You flatter me, Doctor Larkin," she said, forcing herself to speak evenly and pretend that her blush was due to his compliment to her intellect. "And please permit me to apologize, Captain Larkin, for intruding on your grief. It was not my intention, I assure you. My errand was simply to deliver the clothes I had mentioned. I had hoped to accomplish that quickly, but Daphne was very determined to befriend your ward."

"I am afraid that I cannot permit any such apology, Lady Marianne," said the captain with a trace of his usual charming gallantry. "I find myself quite indebted to you this morning. My brother is right in thinking I am more likely to credit an unbiased opinion, besides the analysis of such an intelligent mind as yours."

This time, Marianne's blush really was due to the compliment Captain Larkin paid to her intellect. Although the pleasure of his compliment was diluted by the nagging remembrance that such a quality was as unlikely to endear her to the captain as it was to any other potential suitor.

"And besides, the clothing you have brought is sure to make you the heroine of the day. I am quite possibly the least qualified person in all of England to procure adequate attire for a little girl," he continued with a small, self-deprecating smile. "I daresay, too, that Lady Daphne's presence here today has smoothed over the more awkward moments for both Elizabeth and myself. Elizabeth has been understandably reticent in my company and was significantly more animated and at ease the moment Lady Daphne set out to befriend her."

"That is quite so," agreed his brother. "I believe, I even saw the beginnings of a smile on Elizabeth's face when the two young ladies took their leave of us just now. I should not be at all surprised to find that Lady Daphne's company proves to be a better cure for our new guest than any amount of my own medical expertise."

"I am delighted if Daphne and I are able to be of any service whatsoever. However, it seems our contributions are rather small. I had better collect Daphne though, or else I fear she will entrench herself here for the entirety of the day, but if I have your leave to do so, I will tell Miss Southampton that she is very welcome to visit Daphne and spend as much time in our home as she would like."

"I should be even further indebted to you, Lady Marianne, for I fear that both my brother and I have precious little notion of how to entertain a child, especially a female child," Captain Larkin replied, his gratitude clearly evident.

Marianne made haste to collect Daphne, fearing the captain's gratitude and appreciation were placing her in danger of embracing the confusing fascination she had set aside earlier with such difficulty. Daphne was predictably reluctant to depart, but Marianne remained firm, and succeeded in prying her sister away from her newfound friend, once she assured the two girls that Daphne might call again on the morrow if Elizabeth was sufficiently rested.

CHAPTER 11

When Arabella returned to her girlhood home the next day, rather later in the morning than Marianne had anticipated, Marianne felt as though the sun had finally broken through a thick layer of clouds after days of persistent gloom. With the Earl of Sedgewick having been called into town on business, and Daphne, finding herself incapable of waiting patiently for Arabella's arrival, had taken herself off to call on Elizabeth Southampton a full two hours prior.

Perhaps she was over-dramatizing the event, Marianne thought. She could acknowledge, but that was the nearest and most accurate analogy she could think of. After a breathless and delighted exchange of embraces, she was nearly too happy to sit still and have a dignified conversation. Fortunately, Arabella seemed disinclined to pursue dignified conversational routes herself, and the sisters indulged in a rather chaotic quarter of an hour's laughter and tears.

"I cannot believe how severely I underestimated how much I would miss your presence, dearest," Arabella confided earnestly. "I realized, though, it would have been all but impossible to foresee such a thing simply because we have never been parted for more than a few day's time. I felt as though I were missing my right arm."

"I am glad to hear you say that, for I have been ordering myself not to communicate that same feeling to *you*," laughed Marianne, her spirits lighter than they had been in weeks. She hugged her sister fiercely, relishing the warmth of her and the smell of her perfume. How glad she was that her sister was home, even though she was no longer living the Sedgewick residence.

"Why ever not?"

"Oh, well, I did not wish to dampen your happiness, I suppose, by complaining about how much your absence has saddened me. It seemed selfish."

"Nonsense. I cannot be the only person who thinks it would be far better to be missed than otherwise. I am exceedingly happy to begin my life with Christopher, of course, but it would hurt me immeasurably to think that my absence was of no real significance here," retorted Arabella firmly.

"Well, you have nothing to fear on that account," Marianne reassured her, her voice rueful. "We shall survive, of course, and I know perfectly well that changes like this are both inevitable and necessary. But that knowledge does not seem to make much difference to my feelings."

A flurry of movement in the drawing room doorway caused both sisters to turn at once, expecting to see Daphne burst into the room. Ellen Millworth appeared instead, her face a comical mixture of excitement and apology.

"Ellen," Arabella exclaimed delightedly, rising at once to embrace her friend.

"I am dreadfully sorry. Well, no, I am not *really* all that sorry, or else I would have stayed away, I suppose, but I simply could not wait another moment to see you." Ellen all but babbled, charmingly. "You may order me to leave at once, Marianne, you would be quite right to do so when I am being so selfish and intruding on your reunion with your sister. I would deserve it, and I would trot obediently home, too, but I hope you don't, for all that."

"Of course, I will not order you to leave, you goose. You are family," Marianne assured Ellen. "I, for one, was just wishing that you were here so that we may hear all of Arabella's news and catch her up on the doings in the village at once. Otherwise, everyone will be obligated to repeat things, and details will be forgotten or omitted. This is really much more efficient."

"Count on you to cite efficiency," laughed Ellen.

"I cannot claim that efficiency was even a thought that crossed my mind momentarily," Arabella said, "but now that you mention it, I see that you are correct, of course."

"Besides, with both of us combining our powers of persuasion I suspect we will stand a much better chance of prying out information from *Lady* Willingham," declared Ellen with a look of inexpressible mischief.

Arabella looked certainly pleased with herself at her new title, but Marianne thought it was mostly because she was Lord Willingham's wife, rather than his lady.

"That is certainly bound to be the case," Marianne agreed with Ellen. "And our contrasting styles of interrogation will make it all the more difficult for her to deflect our questions."

"*Lady Willingham*," laughed Arabella, her color high. She looked from Marianne to Ellen. "I assure you, I am Arabella to the two of you. What are you on about?"

"Oh no," said Ellen. "You are a married lady now, and a baroness. Prepare to be interrogated.

"Interrogated?" laughed Arabella. "Whatever can you two mean by that?" But twin spots of color flamed in her cheeks despite her feigned ignorance, Marianne noted.

"Why, we want only want to know what married life is like," Ellen said with an impish smile. "Surely, you will not be too reticent with your sister and your closest friend?"

"Married life is absolutely divine," demurred Arabella, a little cat-like smile forming on her lips. "But that is all that I shall say upon the matter just now, regardless of anyone's superior interrogation tactics. By all means, however, tell me everything that has happened in the village during our absence."

Marianne and Ellen exchanged conspiratorial glances with one another, in perfect accord that they would not let Arabella off of the hook quite so easily. But at just that moment the drawing room door burst open and Daphne along with Elizabeth Southampton in tow, made her characteristic whirlwind entrance.

After exchanging delighted greetings and embraces with Arabella, Daphne recalled the presence of her rather timid looking guest, belatedly introducing her to the new Lady Willingham and explaining that Elizabeth had come along to observe her music lesson.

"Are you fond of music, dear?" asked Marianne kindly, taking the opportunity to study the child's appearance a little. She wore one of Daphne's old frocks, and although the dark blue fabric did little for her pale complexion, the child looked noticeably more rosy and alert.

"Yes, Lady Marianne. I was learning to play the pianoforte a bit before…before we gave up our cottage, that is," answered the girl in her soft voice.

"That will just be another reason for you to come over here a great deal," declared Daphne brightly, dissipating the look of sorrow that had begun to steal back into the other child's face. "For there isn't a pianoforte at the doctor's home, but we have a lovely one here."

"There *isn't* a pianoforte there," Ellen murmured, evidently struck by the realization. "That will never do."

"You are going to marry the doctor, aren't you, Miss Millworth?" asked Elizabeth shyly. "He is a very kind gentleman."

"He certainly is, and yes, I am," laughed Ellen. "I am afraid that is the reason that the doctor's home is in such a state of disarray just now, for it needed a bit of renovation before the wedding."

"I think the renovation is fascinating. Elizabeth and I watched the builders working for quite some time this morning before we returned here," Daphne said, brushing at a bit of sawdust on the hem of her dress. "But now we have just enough time to run and ask Cook for a bite of something before my music lesson."

"Oh, by all means," Marianne said with a smile, "But do your best not to aggravate her, I beg of you, for she has been rather tense lately with the loss of two scullery maids."

The two young girls scampered away, Elizabeth seeming perfectly content to follow Daphne's lead.

"I see there is a great deal of village news to catch me up on, more indeed, than I would have imaged," said Arabella as soon as the door closed behind the pair.

"Do not think that you have put us off forever, Arabella. You are only delaying the inevitable, you know," cautioned Ellen with mock-seriousness.

"Daphne introduced little Miss Southampton as Captain Larkin's ward? I had no idea that he had such a thing," Arabella persisted.

"Neither did he," Ellen replied, conceding defeat temporarily at least. "It was quite a shocking moment when the child arrived. Mama told me that at first she thought it was about to be revealed that poor Captain Larkin had been secretly married or some mistress had given birth.

"Elizabeth is entirely too old for that," Marianne said and then blushed at the thought.

"Well, something of a scandalous nature," added Ellen.

"Captain Larkin strikes me as one of the least likely candidates for a secret marriage, or any sort of scandal, really. He always seems so straightforward and honorable, besides having little concern for convention," mused Arabella thoughtfully. "If he fell in love and married someone shocking, I expect he would have announced it with as much fanfare as if he wed a duchess."

"Mama said Lady Larkin has fretted about that precise thing on more than one occasion," agreed Ellen. "It would be very in keeping with his character. But Miss Southampton is the recently orphaned child of his lieutenant, and dear friend, who sent her, along with a letter of explanation and very little else."

"So that *was* Daphne's old dress the girl was wearing, then. I thought it looked familiar."

"It was, I took a few things over for her to wear until the captain could see about getting her some new clothes of her own," Marianne confirmed, frowning a little. It was somehow both gratifying and irritating to hear Arabella praising Captain Larkin's character, but that thought was not foremost in her mind just then. "But do you know, I suspect he considers the matter over and dealt with."

"It is quite possible that he does," Ellen laughed, rolling her eyes expressively. "You can just imagine that a man would think the child needed clothes, and now she has some, there is nothing more to be done. I quite adore my soon-to-be brother-in-law, you can be sure, but there is no denying his mind is even more ridiculously practical than that of typical gentlemen. It comes from dealing with life and death situations in the military, I suppose."

"Your soon-to-be husband deals with life and death situations in his profession as well," pointed out Arabella as if determined to be fair in the defense of the masculine portion of humanity.

"And as considerate and gentle as Doctor Larkin is, you will notice that *he* has done nothing further to outfit the child either," Marianne argued. "I am not saying either brother is negligent, of course, but I *am* concerned that they seem to not appreciate the full scope of the undertaking, which goes into raising a little girl. And it is not my place to bring such things to the captain's attention, I know that full well. However, I cannot help but worry for the sake of everyone involved. What does a single man know about such things, after all? And what on earth does he intend to do after Ellen and Doctor

Larkin's wedding when he must embark on his next commission? Does he intend to drag the child about the globe with him?"

"Hmm," murmured Arabella, while Ellen seemed to be struggling to master the urge to giggle.

Marianne knew that both Arabella and Ellen were studying her with almost identical curious expressions, almost as if she were a strange insect beneath a magnifying lens. The sensation was exasperating and proved to be more than a match for her equanimity.

"What is it, then?" she demanded, aware of a scowl drawing her brows together as she looked back and forth from one to the other. When neither of her companions answered her, she shifted uneasily in her seat. "Whatever it is you are both evidently thinking, I would much rather hear it than continue to be the subject of such aggravating scrutiny. It is quite maddening."

"Oh, dear, I did not think I was absent for *quite* long enough for the world to be so entirely upended," Arabella said, her eyes dancing with sympathetic laughter. "And yet, here we are with such a perfect reversal of roles that I must have been gone for far longer than I realized."

CHAPTER 12

"Reversal of roles? I wish you would stop speaking in riddles," Marianne retorted, nettled even further by Arabella's comment.

"There, it is that sort of thing exactly." exclaimed Ellen, all but crowing triumphantly. "When, Lady Marianne have you *ever* wished away a nice, baffling riddle? You adore riddles and problems and puzzles of all sorts. It is foundational to your very nature."

Marianne stared at Ellen, quite at a loss for a retort as she registered the accuracy of the comment.

"I only mean, dearest, that in the ordinary course of things it has been Ellen and myself who tend to worry and fret over the actions of others. While we remain largely unaware of the reason for our concern, it has fallen to you to take on the role of being more rational and logical in order to help us see things clearly,"

Arabella said soothingly, taking Marianne's hand in her own in a comforting gesture.

"So I am being… irrational? And unaware of my own reasoning?"

"It does seem that way, although perhaps you are perfectly aware and simply unwilling to communicate your real motives with us?" suggested Ellen with a subdued but still impish smile. She seemed to be enjoying the conversation a great deal, and Marianne suddenly wondered if she had often behaved in an inadvertently infuriating manner herself in the past.

"If this conversation is truly a reversal of our ordinary roles, then I see that I have perhaps behaved rather insufferably in the past," she said stiffly, attempting to sound lighthearted and playful, but admittedly falling short.

"Certainly not," Arabella protested quickly, but Marianne did not miss the sharp, rather quelling look her sister shot at their friend.

"No, you have never been insufferable," agreed Ellen after a brief pause. "Forgive me, Marianne, I did not mean to imply such a thing. It is hardly your fault that I have sometimes been irked by seeing how much slower my own wits are in comparison to yours. I daresay you have always been a great deal more patient and gracious in your superior understanding, but then, you have had a great deal more practice with such a position than I."

"Nonsense," Marianne laughed, much more naturally, at Ellen's words and manner, then added with a sigh. "But it is probably doing me a great deal of good to flounder in such an unfamiliar morass of confusion as I am currently experiencing."

"We would not dream of pressuring you to speak, of course, if you do not wish to," said Arabella virtuously.

"That is fortunate, then, for I still remain more than halfway in the dark about this conversation. Indeed, I am not entirely certain I can say with any certainty whatsoever as to the exact topic this conversation may be. But pray do not feel the need to enlighten me," she added hastily, seeing that Ellen was about to respond. "As you have pointed out, there is nothing in the world that I love so much as a nice, baffling riddle. This certainly fits that description. I was merely expressing my concern for the well-being of an orphaned child, and the two of you started giggling foolishly."

"Indeed," Ellen murmured demurely. Marianne cast back in her mind to recall the exact words that she had used and was struck by an appalling suspicion. Had she inadvertently conveyed some hint of the unfounded emotional reaction that seemed to rear its head anytime she thought of Captain Larkin? That would be mortifying, she thought, but still worse was the possibility that her companions meant something else entirely and she might give away her secret fondness by guessing incorrectly.

Arabella and Ellen showed no sign of breaking the silence that stretched on while Marianne pondered this. After some moments had passed, she had to concede defeat. It would be better to risk exposing her childish fancy than to continue on in ignorance – a state that she had never been able to abide.

"Is it…how I spoke of Captain Larkin?" she ventured, blushing wildly and averting her gaze.

"There you have it," confirmed Arabella in an encouraging voice. "You seem far too infuriated by the captain's short-sightedness, or whatever you would term his attitude, I suppose. Far too infuriated unless you have some other strong emotions rattling around your heart as well, that is."

"I think it would be a false generalization to assume that infuriation is an unfailing symptom of more tender feelings," Marianne hedged, taking temporary refuge in rhetoric.

"Very well then, but does that false generalization prove true in this specific instance?" asked Ellen, meticulously focused.

"I fear it does. But for pity's sake do not breathe a word of this to anyone, not even your fiancé. *Especially* not your fiancé."

"But what is the obstacle, dearest?" asked Arabella curiously. "Captain Larkin is a fine and upstanding gentleman, unattached and quite splendidly handsome. Is it the sudden presence of his ward that you object to?"

"That would be perfectly reasonable, you know. After all, you two have had the raising of yourselves and Daphne from a very early age, and it would be quite understandable if you were not delighted at the prospect of taking on another half-grown child," said Ellen, although a little frown accompanied her words, and Marianne did not think their friend found the idea so very reasonable at all.

"No, that has nothing to do with – with *anything*," Marianne protested quickly. "How could you even arrive at that conjecture when this whole discussion began with my exasperation that the child was not being adequately considered? And besides, it assumes far too much. I am not able to perfectly categorize my own feelings for him, and I suspect that the majority of them stem from a childhood fancy rather than any real, mature regard. Captain Larkin and I have had barely half a dozen conversations with one another. We scarcely can claim to be acquaintances, and besides that, I am certain he has no interest in me."

"Why on earth would you be so certain of that?" wondered Ellen, promptly forgiving Marianne for the imagined slight on her future brother-in-law.

"Well, for one thing, he has given no indication of any interest. And I would be greatly surprised if he, or any other gentleman, for that matter, *did* have any such feelings."

"Marianne Sedgewick, have you taken leave of your senses? You are an exquisitely beautiful and marvelously intelligent young woman of good family and fortune. I daresay you could have your pick of any gentleman upon which you might set your sights," Arabella said, not bothering to conceal her astonishment at Marianne's sentiment.

"Oh, do not mistake me," Marianne replied, smiling at her sister's automatic protest. "I am not saying I am some sort of hideous creature, or entirely without desirable attributes. But I have long accepted the idea that it would be a very rare sort of gentleman indeed who would be capable of truly embracing a wife who engaged in intellectual pursuits. And, I will not have one who would try to dampen my wit. Perhaps you have noticed that gentlemen do not seem to care for a lady challenging their notions of superiority? I have given the matter a great deal of reflection. I do not believe myself capable of feigning stupidity or engaging in the sort of prolonged mental indolence that matrimony would demand. I shall stay right where I am, running the household for Father as best I can, and playing the sisterly chaperone and someday the doting, eccentric aunt. I shall study to my heart's delight, and I will be perfectly content with my lot in life, I am certain."

"If that is truly your choice, and it would truly make you happy, then I will not say another word on the matter," said Arabella, speaking in a slow and rather doubtful tone. "But I hope you will not dismiss at least the possibility of finding a true match, a gentleman who genuinely values your intellect rather than simply tolerating or overlooking it. Surely, the idea that no such male creature exists is another false generalization?"

"Perhaps," Marianne gave a non-committal gesture, breathing a sigh of relief when it seemed the conversation would finally be allowed to take another turn.

"But all of that aside," persisted Ellen suddenly, dashing Marianne's short-lived hopes to be finished with topic once and for all. "And not even examining the fact that you have previously counseled both Arabella and myself against dismissing the possibility of finding true love, you cannot simply ignore your feelings about Captain Larkin, you know."

"But my feelings are entirely irrational, besides being inconsequential. They have no relevance to anything that truly matters. Captain Larkin will stay here until your wedding, and then he will take his leave. Then I suppose, I shall see him once or twice every five years or so due to our family's connections. If the reaction that I seem to have to his presence is based on more than a childhood fancy, it is not as though I will have to deal with it all too often. I do not mean to ignore my feelings, precisely, but I also do not wish to attempt to voice them while they are still so unclear. I do not wish to express them while they are so irrelevant. It is like that line by Publilius Syrus that I insisted Daphne copy over and over once. 'I have often regretted my speech, never my silence.'"

"I have no doubt I could find half a dozen aggravating old Greek philosophers saying the exact opposite of that sentiment, if I had the notion to risk sneezing throughout the afternoon pouring through a stack of dusty volumes," replied Ellen with some asperity.

Publilius Syrus was not a Greek philosopher. He was Roman, well actually, he was originally a Syrian slave, and he wrote sententiae, which is not precisely the same thing as philosophy, you know," Marianne began eagerly, delighted by the prospect of expounding upon one of her favorite topics almost as much as she was delighted by the chance to steer the conversation away from such an irksome subject of her feelings for Captain Larkin, once and for all. It would be remarkably comforting to dwell on more familiar verbal territory, where she was infinitely more sure of her footing, and it was almost as comforting to hear Arabella and Ellen's predictable groans of protest at her lecturing tone. Ellen's eyes seemed to positively glaze over with boredom.

"Providence save us from having to listen to the minute differences between philosophy and sententiae," laughed Arabella, throwing up her hands in defeat. "We yield, we yield, Marianne. Perhaps you would be interested to hear that Christopher and I brought home a very large crate filled with *ancient* scrolls for you that we procured when we stopped in Greece?"

"Truly?" Marianne perked up at once thinking of exploring such a find.

"Truly. Come, you cannot think that I would travel to Greece and not procure some bit of antiquity for you."

"You are the most wonderful sister in the entire world," Marianne declared, hugging her sister. She could actually *feel* her tension and distress evaporate at the prospect of exploring the find.

CHAPTER 13

Marianne had resolved to find a way to enjoy both the intellectual stimulation and the convenient distraction of the literary treasure trove Arabella and Christopher had procured for her *without* neglecting any of her more tedious duties. The undertaking had strained her willpower to its absolute limits, and she could not claim to have maintained perfect success, but some weeks later she was fairly well satisfied with the balance that she had managed to strike.

The contents of the crate had all been carefully examined and sorted, and Marianne had also played hostess for a party of her father's business associates. All while assisting Arabella in entertaining congratulatory rounds of callers. Although she had enjoyed diving into the crate of antiquities a great deal more than she had enjoyed fulfilling her social obligations, Marianne felt a certain sense of accomplishment at having at least marginally succeeded in that area. Even with Elizabeth becoming nearly a fixture at the Sedgewick estate, due to Daphne's enthusiastic friendship, Marianne had been even more successful in fulfilling her resolution to put away her wayward thoughts and feelings regarding the disquieting Captain Larkin. She had the scrolls to thank for that, she knew, since on the occasions when his company had been unavoidable, she had managed easily enough to fix her mind on them instead of any foolishly romantic thoughts.

Feeling virtuous because there was a scroll that had defied her attempts at translation thus far, she was longing desperately to continue poring over it. Instead, Marianne sat down to sort through the pile of correspondence that had been brought in that morning. After reading and replying to several distinctly tedious notes, she came across a missive that caused her to leap from her chair in excitement after the briefest glance.

"Father," she exclaimed, bursting into the earl's study. He raised one iron-grey eyebrow at her with a meaningful expression, and she realized a few seconds too late that her father was not alone in his study. "I beg your pardon, Father, Mr. Baxley."

Mr. Baxley, who was visiting the village rector and had been introduced several nights previously at a dinner party, gave Marianne an indulgent smile and nod.

"Not at all, my dear Lady Marianne. As it happens, your father and I were just speaking of you. Quite complimentary things, I can assure you."

"Oh, indeed? That is always a pleasant surprise," Marianne laughed candidly, her distraction causing her to forget to be quite as politely guarded as she generally preferred to behave around those who she did not know particularly well. Her smile seemed to rather dazzle the middle-aged Mr. Baxley, who blinked at her with a beatific expression which was complimented by a flush of color that went from his cheeks, to his ears, to the top of his bald head.

"Ah, well, Lord Sedgewick, I must compliment your daughter's beauty. She is incomparable."

"My late wife was easily counted the beauty of her day," Lord Sedgewick replied, his manner perfectly bland and unreadable. "Had she lived to see our daughters grown she would have been delighted to see that each has fulfilled her legacy."

"That is such a lovely thing to hear, Father," Marianne said, flushing with pleasure at the rare compliment.

"And moreover, it is quite true, which is more than can be said for the vast majority of compliments," said the earl with an unreadable expression on his handsome, stern visage. For some reason, the gentleman seemed embarrassed by this remark, or at least, he flushed again and turned his eyes away for a moment.

"Well, if you will forgive me for interrupting your conversation, Father, I did have some significant news to relate. It is significant to me, at least," said Marianne, taking advantage of the short and mysterious lull in the conversation.

"Any news of importance to yourself must certainly take precedence over all else," said the gentleman gallantly, seeming to recover himself although from what, Marianne could not begin to fathom.

"Yes, of course, what was it that you rushed in here to tell me?" said Lord Sedgewick, and there was a distinctly nettled quality to his voice.

"Perhaps you recall that Arabella and Christopher brought back a crate of scrolls from Greece?" she forged ahead, too excited about her news to puzzle any longer over the strange tension that filled the room. Her father only nodded his acknowledgement, so she continued. "I have been working on them, you know; categorizing them and sorting through their contents, translating them if they are unfamiliar. Well, one was rather a mystery to me. I thought that I could identify the author by the style, yet I have never come across this particular writing before, which is odd because I thought I had familiarized myself with all of his works."

"Certainly, my dear," interjected her father in a tone that was clearly intended to recall Marianne before she went too far on an academic tangent, she knew.

"I wrote to a scholar from Oxford University, a gentleman who is quite the expert in this specific branch of antiquities, hoping that he might help me clarify the matter. He has written back saying that it seems possible I have discovered an unknown work of Hesiod, which would of course have really very important ramifications, you know."

"That is exciting news indeed, I understand," Lord Sedgewick nodded indulgently. Marianne suspected that he would have had precisely the same manner if she had been excited over a new hat, or in her younger years, a doll, or a flower, abstractly pleased for her happiness over something that he personally cared little about.

"Ah, yes, I must say, since our last meeting, I've been considering how very well-educated and bright you are, Lady Marianne," added Mr. Baxley. "Do you mean to tell me that you are actually well-versed enough in the Greek language to make an attempt at translating it on your own?"

"Oh, why yes. I have always adored learning scholarly languages," Marianne admitted cautiously. The gentleman sounded somewhat condescending and she remembered how appalled he seemed previously. Now, he was feigning interest in her intellect, which he clearly did not appreciate. He looked as though he did not quite believe her ability, but she had neither the time or the inclination to correct him. "But Father, as excited as I am by the possibility of having made such a significant discovery, that is not what I was rushing in here to tell you. In his letter, Sir Downing, that is the name of the scholar from Oxford, did I mention his name already? Sir Theodore Downing writes he is about to leave Oxford for a brief amount of time and as his travels will bring him quite near to our village, he intends to stop here in order to examine the scroll personally."

"Indeed, and I imagine it is a very wise course of action to have such an artifact studied by a real expert," Mr.

Baxley put in, and there was no mistaking the note of condescension present in his voice. Marianne spared the gentleman a brief, irritated glance, but did not bother to point out that she herself might be considered a *real expert* in the matter.

"Sir Downing's credentials are quite impressive," she replied instead, straining for any amount of patience and tact that she could manage. "My excitement, or rather, I should say, my sense of urgency, stems not from that fact but from the unfortunate fact that Sir Downing's letter was delayed somehow and the date that he suggests he will arrive here is *today*."

"Ah, all becomes clear, my dear," Lord Sedgewick declared with an air of satisfied comprehension.

"I do apologize, Father, for the short notice."

"You can hardly take responsibility for the deplorable state of our country's postal service. I daresay our hospitality will not be strained by an unexpected visitor here and there. Your sister and her husband were planning to dine here this evening, weren't they? So, this Sir Downing may join us all if he arrives today without it being too great of a shock to the cook," Her father said. "Oh, ah, and your presence would be welcome as well, Baxley," added the earl as a hasty afterthought.

It was clear to Marianne that her father's tactic of ignoring the man's presence had backfired, for he had forgotten Mr. Baxley was listening until good manners forced her father to extend an invitation. She expected the man to decline the invitation, as it had so obviously been given out of mere politeness, but to her surprise he simply beamed a rather foolish smile.

"Why, nothing should delight me more, Lord Sedgewick. We can perhaps continue our delicate conversation further after sharing a meal. I shall bid you a temporary farewell, and you as well, Lady Marianne, although I doubt, I should be able to bear the parting if I were not promised a speedy return."

"Good afternoon, Mr. Baxley," Marianne managed to say as the man bowed deeply and cast a significant look her way before departing.

Her father scowled at the door as it closed behind the gentleman, then shook his head and sighed. "Well, that certainly wasn't the response I had hoped for."

"What did he want, Father? He had such an odd air about him, it was quite mystifying. And whatever did he mean by continuing your delicate conversation? I would not pry, or at least, I would attempt to not pry quite so openly, if he had some sort of long-time association with you. But I was under the impression that the man was only recently introduced," Marianne did her best to pitch her voice softly, on the chance that Mr. Baxley had not moved beyond earshot. For some reason it struck her as the sort of thing the man might do, although she could hardly have said why she felt that way.

"You are quite right, and as for what Mr. Baxley wants, I fear I do not have the patience to put the matter tactfully at the moment, so I will say in short that he appears to be in want of a wife."

"He is as likely as any other gentleman to find one, I suppose," said Marianne, still terribly bewildered. "But why on earth would he think that *you* could assist him in such an enterprise?"

"Really, Marianne, if I did not know any better, I might wonder if you have filled your mind so entirely with dead languages and mathematical figures that you have perhaps crowded out any common sense. How do you *think* I might assist him in that particular venture? I, a man blessed with a beautiful and unattached, to say nothing of wealthy, daughter of marrying age?" demanded Lord Sedgewick with some asperity.

"Oh," gasped Marianne, completely taken aback by the idea, although she supposed her father was right in thinking she ought to have pieced it together without assistance. She struggled for a moment to bring back to her mind an image of Mr. Baxley, his middle-aged face with its overly fond smile, his irritatingly paternal tone of voice. She could not suppress the irreverent giggle that bubbled into her throat. "Me?"

"I take it that you are disinclined to encourage the gentleman's advances, then?" her father asked with a humorously dry tone of voice. "In that case I may rest assured you still have at least *some* modicum of common sense remaining. The man is a ridiculous fool, there is no other way to put it. The nerve of maneuvering himself into an introduction for no other purpose than to flatter his way into my favor so he might pursue you."

"But why would he go to all of that trouble? We have no connection to him, after all."

"Ah, well, it seems Mr. Baxley does not want to participate in such a tawdry affair as the London Season; yet, nothing will do for him but a young, beautiful, and wealthy bride, so he has taken to gathering suggestions from his underlings. It is hardly a surprise that your name was mentioned, my dear, but rather annoying all the same."

"Rather," Marianne agreed, regaining her sense of humor after a brief pause. "I thought my intellect discouraged him well enough previously.

Apparently, he has reconsidered since the dinner party. He has decided that you would be able to provide him with handsome and intelligent sons."

Marianne snorted with laughter. "Not if they were to take after their father! Well, I hope he has several other options for a broodmare, since he is doomed to disappointment if he has pinned all of his hopes here."

"Doubtless he will survive the disappointment, although I fancy he will be quite astonished by it," Father said.

"I expect he can withstand a little astonishment, a hypothesis which we can begin testing this very evening, apparently."

CHAPTER 14

Marianne sent Daphne with a note to Arabella, realizing that she would never be able to pull off the impromptu dinner gathering at such short notice without some expert assistance. Besides, she was far too distracted to attend to all the fussy, but necessary, little details demanded of a hostess. Her mind was split between a sort of horrified amusement at her father's revelation about Mr. Baxley's intentions, and purely academic delight at the prospect of discussing her little treasure trove with a true expert.

Arabella answered her summons quite promptly and took the measure of the situation in one practiced glance. "Go up and dress for dinner now, Marianne, since we do not know precisely when your visitor will arrive. I'll see about adjusting the menu and freshening up the settings a bit," she said briskly.

"I'm awfully sorry to send for you like this," Marianne began, speaking quickly for she knew perfectly well that her sister was unlikely to listen to her apology.

"Nonsense, you know I am quite happy to come and lend a hand," Arabella laughed, giving her a gentle shove in the direction of the stairs. "Mind that you keep from running your fingers through your hair once it has been attended to. I could see from halfway up the drive that you've been doing precious little else all the forenoon."

"I shall do my best," Marianne said ruefully as she started up the staircase. "It never seems to be of much use, however. My fingers seem to muss it of their own accord."

By the time she was properly attired, and her hair was secured with so many pins that it might actually stand a chance of staying in place regardless of her careless habit, Arabella had apparently worked a small miracle. The entire atmosphere of the house seemed lighter and more productive than it had in months. No amount of studying, Marianne decided, would ever replace her sister's innate ability to manage the household staff. Rather than feel depressed by the realization, she determined to simply feel grateful for the temporary improvement.

"Oh, there you are, Marianne." Daphne appeared at the foot of the stairs, fairly bouncing with excitement, and accompanied by Elizabeth as had become the usual state of affairs in the past few weeks. "You look simply marvelous, and it is a good thing, too."

"Why, particularly?" Marianne wondered, bemused by the younger girl's drolly significant tone.

"Your guest of honor has arrived, not ten minutes ago, and he is *extremely* handsome, isn't he, Elizabeth? I daresay you didn't know that about him, for he certainly seems to know very little about *you*," replied Daphne, with an expression of barely suppressed mirth.

"That is true enough, we have only corresponded, and not about anything particularly personal, from what I can recall. Just about antiquities and things like that."

"I believe you," giggled Daphne, causing Marianne to stop in her tracks to peer suspiciously into her sister's face. "No, it is no use looking as though you are trying to read my mind, I will give nothing away, and neither will Elizabeth. You will just have to come into the drawing room and see for yourself."

"Very well," conceded Marianne, shaking her head at this new folly of Daphne's.

She proceeded directly to the drawing room, doing her best to ignore Daphne's bouncing energy and move at a more dignified pace, although her excitement at speaking with the expert was certainly heightened. Daphne darted ahead to fling open the door to the drawing room in a dramatic fashion and declare grandly, "Sir Henry Downing, may I present to you M. Sedgewick, otherwise known as Lady *Marianne* Sedgewick."

"Oh, really, Daphne," Marianne began, wondering why Arabella was not there to remind the child of her manners, but her protest died upon her lips as she took in the sight of the Oxford scholar.

He had risen automatically, but seemed to be frozen in a sort of momentary shock as he looked back at her. Marianne realized she had been picturing the gentleman quite incorrectly for the entirety of their correspondence since he bore absolutely no resemblance to the bent, gray scholar she had always imagined.

Instead, Sir Henry was tall and extraordinarily handsome, with dark hair brushed back from his brow, and somehow luminous gray eyes. He did possess the pallor she associated with lifelong scholars, but the pale complexion suited him perfectly and only accented his wonderfully chiseled looking features. He looked like nothing so much as a perfect marble statue come to life, she thought distractedly. But although his appearance explained her own confused reaction, Marianne realized she still had no explanation for his own evident confusion.

"*You* are M. Sedgewick?" he asked, suddenly finding his voice, if not his good manners.

"Ah, yes?" she replied, feeling a blush rise to her cheeks at his surprise. Was there something amiss with her appearance, she wondered, trying to recall her last hasty glance in the looking glass before leaving her chamber.

"I beg your pardon, that sounded terribly rude," Sir Henry said, a slight blush lending color to his own face. "You must forgive me, though. I have been under the impression that I was corresponding with er, a gentleman, and I fear that I am quite at a loss to adjust my ideas."

"A gentleman? *Oh*," Marianne gasped with the sudden, dawning realization that struck her. "Oh, dear, I do apologize, Sir Henry. The mistake is entirely my fault, but I assure you that I did not intend to deliberately mislead you. I have been in the habit for some years now of signing my letters M. Sedgewick whenever I write to a fellow schola or, that is, not a *fellow* scholar, as I have never studied formally, perhaps I would do better to say a person who shares some of my same interests, yet that seems terribly vague…"

Her voice trailing off in confusion, Marianne felt utterly wretched. Sir Henry's expression was entirely unreadable, and she could not determine whether he felt angry or amused by the ridiculous situation. Taking a steadying breath, she composed her thoughts and ordered herself to speak with a little more precision and focus. She sounded like a simpering miss, which she was most certainly not. She began again with aplomb.

"What I mean to say, Sir Henry is that whenever I write a letter in the nature of a scholarly inquiry, such as my missive to you a few weeks back, I am in the habit of signing my correspondence as M. Sedgewick. I have found that my questions are taken much more seriously and in fact, are actually answered if I do not volunteer the fact that I am a lady. I would have clarified the issue in our correspondence before your arrival, had your letter not unfortunately been delayed. It did not arrive until earlier today, and I am afraid that in my excitement and haste to prepare for your imminent arrival, the detail slipped my mind entirely. I apologize most sincerely for the confusion, sir, as well as for my younger sister's woeful lack of tact," she concluded, aiming a quick glance of approbation in Daphne's unrepentant direction. The girl looked as if she might break into giggles at any moment if Marianne could assess the bright sparkle in her eyes.

"Both of which apologies are quite unnecessary, I assure you, ah, *Lady* Marianne, is it? Sir Henry replied, gallant if still rather uncertain of his ground.

At Marianne's quick nod of assent, he continued speaking. "I have a younger sister of my own, and I do not imagine for one moment that she would be able to resist gleefully perpetuating such a Shakespearian misunderstanding for the sake of her own amusement. As a matter of fact, I daresay that most of us would find a great deal of humor in witnessing such a thing unfold.

As for the other matter, it is *I* who must apologize, it seems. I had no idea that my letter was delayed, for I wrote it just as I was about to set out on my travels and never looked for a reply. I am afraid that in my excitement over your findings I quite overlooked practicalities, which is an unfortunate tendency of mine, I must confess. You might have been traveling yourself, or ill, or otherwise unable to receive visitors, and at the very least I am certain that my unexpected arrival has been something of an inconvenience."

"Oh, no, I assure you that I was quite delighted to receive your letter this morning," replied Marianne earnestly. "I have been quite unable to put the mystery of this particular scroll out of my mind, you know, and my thoughts *will* keep drifting back to it no matter how determinedly I set them upon other courses. It will be such a relief to have the wretched thing properly identified by an expert."

"Lady Marianne, I should say that based upon the content of our correspondence thus far I would term *you* an expert in this matter," Sir Henry said, with all appearances of sincerity. Marianne felt a pleased glow at the compliment, for she could not detect a trace of flattery or condescension in the gentleman's manner. She found the gentleman's words unutterably appealing.

"Why, no," she murmured, feeling remarkably flustered. "That is, I have not been formally trained or educated or anything of the sort. I am very glad to have someone with your credentials to look at the scroll."

"The fact that you possess such a wealth and depth of knowledge without having received the benefit of formal education is all the more impressive, if you ask me," he countered. "Indeed, the thought of what you might have accomplished with such training is fairly amazing, and I suspect it might have some bearing on the poor quality of responses that you received from scholars who were aware that you are *Lady Marianne* rather than Mr. Sedgewick.

"I am afraid that many of my colleagues have a tendency to be rather vain, and therefore, rather insecure as regards their intellectual superiority. I have found my youth is a similar liability in conversation. They do not take kindly to having their prior notions threatened, and a mind as sharp as yours might be rather intimidating."

"It is of little consequence to me, really, or at least, it has ceased to be," Marianne said candidly waving off the comment. "Perhaps I once did feel rather irritated by such things, but all in all I am quite privileged to be able to read and study to my heart's content without having to jockey for position amongst a great crowd of scholars."

This statement was almost entirely true, although she could not deny the occasional pang of longing at the thought of an energetic and stimulating exchange of ideas with fellow scholars. Perhaps Sir Henry caught something in her tone that gave her away, for he gave her a shrewd and rather sympathetic glance. He looked as though he might say something else on the topic, but Arabella entered the room at that moment.

"A thousand apologies, Sir Henry, for rushing away in such an abrupt manner," she declared in a light and merry tone that had the slightest hint of an edge to it, detectable only to someone very familiar with her, Marianne thought. "There was a very minor domestic catastrophe, I am afraid, that needed my attention right away, but all is set to rights now."

"Think nothing of it, Lady Willingham. Your younger sister has attended to me with all due hospitality," he replied graciously, if untruthfully. Marianne could not quite suppress a snort at the gentleman's words, but she masked the noise quickly in a sort of cough. She had not offered the man a cup or tea or so much as a seat, so intent was she on the scroll and the possibilities it lent.

"I feared as much," Arabella said ruefully, throwing Marianne a glance. "Which is precisely the reason that I hurried back as quickly as I could. Well, that, and my fear that Marianne would be unable to refrain from dragging you directly to the library before you could so much as catch your breath. Won't you come and refresh yourself? I have ordered tea and cakes to tide us over until supper."

"It *has* been rather a strain on my self-control, but see how wonderfully I have managed thus far," Marianne rejoined cheerfully enough, for Sir Henry had met her eyes with a rather conspiratorial smile at the suggestion. "I did not drag the man into the library for my amusement." A blush heated Marianne's face at the unintended innuendo, but Sir Henry seemed not to notice.

"I am afraid that social conventions and niceties have very little consideration for the desires of the academic mind, so having resigned myself to waiting to inspect the scroll I would have been quite delighted to be ordered thus," he declared, with a slight smile directed her way. Marianne felt an unaccustomed warm and happy glow at the gentleman's regard or perhaps it was just the heat of her blush on her cheeks.

PART III

CHAPTER 15

The remainder of the dinner guests arrived shortly thereafter, and Marianne found that her enjoyment of Sir Henry's presence was such that she even forgot her baffled irritation at Mr. Baxley at least, for the most part. In all honesty, she had forgotten that the ridiculous man had accepted his lukewarm invitation to dinner, and had nearly forgotten that he existed altogether until his arrival.

It was almost comical to see the way his beaming, condescending smile slipped by several very noticeable degrees upon his introduction to Sir Henry. Evidently the gentleman was less than pleased with the dashing appearance of the new arrival. Still less did he seem to care for Marianne's animated conversation with the scholar all during the meal, which left all and sundry behind in confusion. Marianne could not bring herself to be overly troubled by such a minor consideration, particularly since Mr. Baxley continued to take every possible opportunity to pay her unwelcome and simpering compliments. Instead, she briefly told the story of how her signing M. Sedgewick had caused some confusion.

"I, for one, cannot begin to imagine mistaking such a paragon of femininity as Lady Marianne here for anything other than a lady," he declared once the story had been related to the assembled party and the resulting laughter had died down. "Not even in written communication, for surely the graceful beauty of penmanship and the delicate eloquence that is so characteristic of the gentler sex would be quite exceedingly obvious. I suppose it is a mark of your admirable single-minded focus on academic topics, Sir Henry, that you did not notice. Indeed, it is quite to your credit as an Oxford scholar."

"I do not believe that I have ever had the privilege of corresponding with you, sir," Marianne said, after a momentary pause during which time she digested the poorly veiled insult to her guest. "If I had, you would know that it is hardly Sir Henry fault for not guessing my true nature, for my penmanship has ever been woefully unlovely."

"I can vouch for that," Lord Willingham agreed, wiping tears of mirth from his eyes. He had found the anecdote endlessly amusing as he was aware of Marianne's foibles. "Marianne's writing always seems to reflect the fact that her mind works at a great deal faster rate than any mortal pen could possibly hope to attain. It is quite legible, of course, but she certainly wastes no time on the more purely aesthetic aspects of penmanship."

"That is entirely accurate, and was indeed the despair of our governesses," Arabella added with a fond smile of reminiscence.

"If mankind ever manages to create a more rapid and efficient system of writing then I, for one, will be forever grateful," Sir Henry said in a mild tone, clearly not about to rise to Mr. Baxley's pointless insult. "I do not claim that my own thoughts are necessarily very rapid, but my writing is dreadfully slow."

"Do you think such a thing could ever be accomplished?" Marianne wondered, distracted entirely by the fascinating notion. "Not another system of letters, I mean, but something else altogether that would allow for faster writing. Something like the device invented by Mr. Turri for his blind friend in Italy."

"I cannot see why such a thing would be necessary for a sighted person," Arabella said. "After all, if I remember your commentary on the device, it was invented because the blind cannot see the letters, but can feel the keys of the device."

"It would eliminate cramped fingers," Marianne added.

"Why would anyone need to write so much?" Mr. Baxley wondered and Marianne considered referencing the possibilities, but she decided against bringing up the topic, and instead turned back to Sir Henry. "Nonetheless, I think it would be a marvelous invention if someone could find a way forward. Don't you think so, Sir Henry?"

"As I have focused all of my energies and attentions on the realm of historical studies, I am scarcely qualified to so much as guess at such a thing. But I daresay it is fair enough to say that no true historian would ever rule out the possibility of any aspect of human ingenuity. The resourceful solutions of even the most primitive of ancient societies makes that case clearly enough," replied Sir Henry, and Marianne could not resist the temptation of asking him for specific examples, even though the conversation was perhaps less fascinating to the rest of the dinner guests.

※

"Why on earth is poor Mr. Baxley looking so perturbed?" Arabella demanded in a discrete whisper as the ladies left the gentlemen at the conclusion of the meal. "He does not seem nearly so well-pleased with himself as he struck me when I first met him."

"I do not know which you will find more difficult to believe; my answer, or that I failed to mention it to you when you first arrived to help," laughed Marianne with a shake of her head. In truth, she had simply not been able to devote much time to thinking about the man's bizarre intentions, having been so focused on the Greek papers and preparing for the arrival of Sir Henry Downing.

"I suspected there must be some greater explanation for his presence here this evening than the one I was given. But you have been understandably distracted today, and I did not have any time to spare to press you for more details."

"In short, in *very* short, for I do not trust Daphne with this information at the moment, given her recent decision to prize humor over manners," Marianne whispered to her elder sister. "The gentleman is in search of a wife and came here to visit with the express purpose of maneuvering an introduction to our family. Having accomplished that last week, and being favorably impressed with me, I must assume, he called on Father today to announce his intentions."

Arabella stopped in her tracks. "That cannot possibly be true," Arabella stated, surprised into speaking with a great deal more bluntness than was her usual custom. "Not that Mr. Baxley was favorably impressed with you, of course," she added quickly when Marianne laughed at the accidental implication. "Of course, he was, any man with eyes in his head would be, you know that. But why ever would he imagine that you or Father, either of you, would entertain the notion of such a match?"

"I really cannot say that I have had any time to dissect the man's psyche and thought processes. I only just discovered this development today, and I have spared little thought for it. Father seemed quite obviously annoyed by the conversation, and yet I did not notice that Mr. Baxley perceived any degree of Father's irritation, so I would venture to guess that he is not the sort of gentleman who is burdened with an overabundance of awareness. From what Father has told me, albeit briefly, the man has quite a specific list of qualities he is seeking in a bride, and it may not have occurred to him that most potential mates are likely to have their own such lists."

"He would not be particularly unique in his mindset if that is the case," Arabella said. "I have noticed that the vast majority of gentlemen are quite startled to find that ladies have opinions and desires of their own. Am I safe in assuming that the misguided man does not meet your own personal criteria for a suitor?"

Marianne snorted. "That might be one of the safest assumptions that could possibly be made," Marianne said, shaking her head and giving a tiny shudder. "On the basis of only the briefest of acquaintances I can say with certainty that the gentleman and I would be monstrously ill-matched even without the great discrepancy in our ages."

"And that discrepancy alone is practically insurmountable, although I daresay such matches are not unheard of. But really, he must be nearly the same age as Father." Arabella's voice rose a little in indignation, but she quickly subsided when she noticed Daphne and Elizabeth looking decidedly curious.

"Never mind any of that," said Marianne. "I am far more interested in hearing what domestic catastrophe called you away so urgently that you were forced to leave our poor guest to Daphne's mercy," said Marianne, neatly changing the subject and quelling Daphne's interest in eavesdropping at the same time. The girl glanced away hurriedly and began to tug her friend towards the relative safety of the pianoforte.

"You'll not escape a scolding, my dear," Arabella called teasingly to Daphne. "You might merely delay it a while longer."

Marianne had a moment's wonder at the change that marriage had wrought in her older sister. There had been a time not so very long ago when such an ill-mannered escapade would have caused Arabella a great deal of distress and frustration, but today she was smiling. Such was the influence of love, she thought with a sigh, for Arabella was very much in love with her new husband. "And do not think that a delay will soften my temper, either," Marianne added in a rather sterner tone.

"It might dilute your attention, however," murmured Arabella. "And I imagine that our sweet little sister is counting on just that. But you wanted to know what called me away earlier? It was perhaps a bit of an overstatement to term the event a catastrophe, but it *was* rather distressing all the same. No less than two maids gave their notice quite abruptly, right as the staff was in the middle of preparations for the evening. You can imagine it threw quite a few things off rather badly, but everyone managed to regain their equilibrium. The housekeeper will begin looking for replacements as soon as she is able, so there is no real need for you to worry, dear."

"We really have been having the worst luck with keeping maids ever since you left," Marianne said, taking her seat with a discouraged sigh. "I know I must be doing something wrong, but for the life of me I cannot think what it is."

"Do not blame yourself too much, for there was certainly plenty of turnover before my marriage. I suspect it simply did not register with you very often because it was not a part of your daily concerns to oversee the household," Arabella pointed out kindly, but Marianne shook her head.

"It isn't that, or at least, it is not *only* that. There is such a great many undercurrents and rivalries and hierarchy. I cannot seem to make sense of it enough to keep from offending at least one portion of the staff on a daily basis. It seems one or another of the maids is constantly bickering and spiteful with another. At the risk of sounding completely uncharitable of my own sex, I wish Father would allow the hiring of more men in the household even though with the tax, footmen are more costly than maids. If it would not mitigate the pecking order or the women, it might at least diversify the problem.

"You make it sound as though you were attempting to unravel the inner workings of some mysterious ancient society," her sister teased gently.

"I daresay I would find *that* a far more enjoyable task." Marianne confessed.

CHAPTER 16

When the gentlemen rejoined the ladies in the drawing room Marianne was listening intently to Arabella, who was painstakingly explaining the finer nuances of the interactions among the household staff. She found that if she could at least *pretend* to be studying the social structure of a historical civilization, then it was noticeably easier to pay careful attention to Arabella's explanations. Nevertheless, she was glad enough for the interruption that the arrival of the gentlemen provided, until Mr. Baxley made an obvious and very determined beeline for her.

"Dearest Lady Marianne, Lady Willingham, I hope you will both pardon my intrusion into what seems to be a decidedly absorbing conversation," the gentleman said, taking a seat that was several shades too near to Marianne for her taste. "If I were to venture a guess as to the topic, I would say that perhaps you are speaking of romance and beau? I understand that there is nothing more fascinating to the mind of a young lady."

"I cannot claim that I spare very much thought for romance and beau, personally," Marianne replied, doing her best to avoid her sister's eyes for she knew Arabella was perilously close to an outburst of either merriment or annoyance. "As a matter of fact, sir, we were discussing the best course of action in managing household staff."

"Ah, wonderful," said the gentleman with an ingratiating smile. "There is nothing more proper, in my opinion, than a woman who is devoted to the smooth running of her home. It is a great pity that more young ladies are not so devoted to their natural calling as you are, Lady Marianne. And I understand that you have the responsibility of managing your father's household resting solely upon your delicate shoulders?"

"Unfortunately for my father's household, yes," laughed Marianne, unable to keep a serious expression no matter how she might try. The idea of being cast as a sort of model domestic creature was simply too absurd. "I am perhaps the least capable manager that there is. I daresay my younger sister Daphne would do a better job, but I would not wish such monotonous drudgery upon her, most days, at least. The truth is that I am woefully unsuited to my natural calling, as you term it, and have just been throwing myself upon the mercy of Lady Willingham to repeat some explanations and words of wisdom on the matter yet again. I do not say so for the sake of sounding modest," she added, recalling her previous difficulty in getting Mr. Baxley to believe her. If the man persisted in his obstinacy, he might insist upon her creating a menu or approving a floral arrangement on the spot.

"My sister is the fortunate possessor of a brilliant intellect which would be the envy of any university scholar," Arabella added rather hastily, perhaps concerned with the forceful tone which Marianne employed at the end of her speech. "Her mind is so often absorbed with complicated academic matters that such mundane routines cannot hope to compete."

"I have heard of your keen wits, of course, Lady Marianne," said Mr. Baxley recovering his smooth and patronizing manner after a moment of seeming nonplussed at the unexpected turn in the conversation. "And I have been enchanted by the display of your intelligent discourse on such a varied array of topics this evening. Pray do not be embarrassed, or worry that such qualities will make you any less desirable to me, my dear. Any true gentleman is willing to wink at a few such charming little faults, you know."

Marianne bristled slightly at have her intellect be called a fault, but she held her tongue as he continued.

"And besides that, I believe that a man of discretion and foresight ought to take pains to secure a wise mother for his future sons."

"Indeed? And you are quite certain that my intellect does not render me entirely repulsive?" asked Marianne sweetly, ignoring Arabella's sharp intake of breath at the man's outrageous statement. "Oh, certainly not. Your beauty and charm more than make up for any such, ah, deficits. It would be impossible to think that *you* are unwomanly. After all, I very much doubt that any great harm can come from a predisposition to reading and studying, particularly when those interests are guided by a wise and benevolent instructor," assured Mr. Baxley, his smile making it clear that he would gladly cast himself in the role of instructor.

"Ah, Mr. Baxley, I wonder if you would be so gracious as to allow me to intrude on your conversation for a moment," said Sir Henry.

Marianne lost the thread of the biting response that she had just been about to make to the man as she looked into the rather dazzling eyes of Sir Henry, who had approached unnoticed, along with her brother-in-law.

"Certainly, certainly," replied the older man in a tone of false heartiness. He clearly resented the intrusion, unaware of the fact that it saved him from a scathing diatribe from the lady in question.

"You have my sincere gratitude, and I shall do my best to keep from monopolizing Lady Marianne's time, but I fear that my self-control and patience has reached its absolute limit. Lady Marianne, do you think that we have paid our dues to good manners and conventional behavior fully enough that you might now allow me to examine the Hesiod scroll?"

Marianne could have kissed Sir Henry on the spot, his good looks, not withstanding.

"I should certainly hope so, for there is nothing that *I* would rather do. But I must defer to my sister's ruling on the case, for her knowledge of how to fulfil social conventions is fathoms beyond my own," said Marianne, a little surprised to find that a smile could break through her annoyance.

"I daresay you have behaved properly and patiently enough, after all, examining that scroll is the whole purpose of Sir Henry's visit. It might be poor manners to delay him any longer," Arabella answered, looking both disappointed and relieved that Mr. Baxley would not be put in his place just then.

"In that case, I apologize for my rudeness, Sir Henry," Marianne said. "The scroll is in our library, and I do not like to move it more than is absolutely necessary for fear of damaging it. I have kept it out of direct sunlight, of course, due to its fragility and age, but even so I believe it has deteriorated slightly in the course of my own examination. Will you come this way?"

"Ah, Mr. Baxley, perhaps you can tell me something of your home," said Lord Willingham, promptly interpreting and obeying the sharp look that Arabella shot at him. "I believe you hail from Derbyshire originally? I have heard marvelous things about a strain of horses that have been bred there, and I have been thinking of making a journey to see for myself."

"I am afraid that I know very little about horses," began the gentleman, but Arabella sailed gracefully over the man's objection.

"Oh, splendid. Do not be modest, Mr. Baxley, I am sure you know a great deal, for I have yet to meet a gentleman who was *not* thoroughly well-versed on the matter. It is so *quintessentially masculine*, I suppose, knowledge of horses. You can tell my husband all about the Derbyshire horses and keep him entertained while I accompany my sister to the library. I daresay you two will have barely scratched the surface of the matter before we return."

His masculinity called into question; Mr. Baxley was unable to think of a way to escape. Although Marianne could tell from his darting expression that he certainly made an attempt, but was promptly subjected to a volley of questions on equine husbandry practices. Arabella shot her husband a grateful look as he rose to the challenge.

"My goodness, Arabella, that was neatly done. A trifle vicious, but neatly done all the same," Marianne murmured once the trio had made their escape. "And I owe Christopher my eternal gratitude, for I know he is making a great sacrifice for my sake."

"He certainly is," Arabella laughed shortly. "For I can tell you that his passion for horses is not a match for his low tolerance of unpleasant company. His fondness for his sister-in-law and his wife, however, trumps all, I am happy to say. As for my being vicious, I offer no excuse or apology. I will certainly not idly tolerate someone insulting my sister in such an odious manner."

"Upon reflection, I daresay Mr. Baxley did not intend to give offence, no matter how insulting he seemed. But it is hardly to his credit, for I have the distinct impression that he is not aware that a woman could be insulted by such comments," Marianne said.

"My inquisitive nature, and lack of manners, compels me to ask what exactly Mr. Baxley was saying?" wondered Sir Henry, glancing from one sister to the other with avid curiosity.

"The lack of manners is all ours, I fear," said Arabella with a little sigh. Before she had fallen in love and married Lord Willingham, she had been a great deal more concerned with propriety. Marianne supposed that the old habit would never really leave, even if her sister momentarily relaxed her standards of decorum now and then.

"The gentleman was just reassuring me that my intellect does not necessarily make me undesirable, for I possess desirable qualities that offset that defect. Besides which, a judicious husband will evidently be able to simultaneously overlook and correct my shortcomings," Marianne supplied, feeling rather oddly embarrassed to be relating such information to Sir Henry, but curious nonetheless to see how he might react.

"And yet he still lives?" wondered the scholar humorously, his eyes widening in mock amazement. He waited a moment, while the two sisters laughed at his comment, then continued in a much softer, more serious tone. "Lady Marianne, I will presume upon our short acquaintance, given the length of our correspondence, enough to say that I hope you do not credit that gentleman's comments for even the slightest of moments. For while it is true that you certainly do possess a great many desirable attributes, it is your intellect that I, for one, find exceedingly compelling…and attractive."

Marianne blinked at him, for once, entirely without words to counter his comment.

CHAPTER 17

"I shall just be over here, I believe I left a novel that I did not have time to finish reading before my wedding," Arabella declared, bustling ostentatiously away from Marianne and her guest, in the humming silence that followed Sir Henry's statement.

In confusion, Marianne could genuinely think of nothing to say in response to Sir Henry. The compliment rang of sincerity, and the admiration in his tone was unmistakable, even someone as inexperienced as she could see that. The very idea of being desired for her intelligence rather than for the more superficial reasons that drew Mr. Baxley and his ilk was so unexpected and foreign that she could scarcely wrap her mind around it, which was ironic, she supposed irrelevantly.

"Forgive me if I misspoke, Lady Marianne," Sir Henry murmured before she could distract herself any further. "I meant no offence or impropriety, I assure you."

"Of course not, that is, there is nothing to forgive. I suppose I should thank you. How remiss of me! I simply had no idea how to respond to your sentiments, for I have never before heard them uttered. Although generally speaking, the matter is not put quite so tactlessly as Mr. Baxley managed, his line of thinking is far from unusual, you must surely know."

"I suppose that is true, and yet like so many other aspects of our civilized society, I believe I shall never fail to be baffled by that particular attitude."

"And yet, there is really nothing to be accomplished by railing against it, or even by snubbing individual gentlemen, although I must say, there is a great deal of satisfaction in seeing it done so skillfully as Arabella managed," laughed Marianne ruefully.

"I should not care to be on the receiving end of her ire, nor that of any member of this family, I think. From what I have seen in just one evening, the earl's daughters are indeed formidable."

"We are at that, I suppose, although we tend to reserve that description for Daphne. Here is the scroll in question, and I shall do my very best to keep from hanging over you like an anxious parent while you examine it, which may exhaust my own supply of self-control, I must admit."

"It will not bother me in the slightest if you do hover, for I have been told on numerous occasions that I would not be disturbed by a hurricane or a thundering herd of elephants if my attention were fixed upon an academic task, and certainly, I should not be disturbed by a fellow scholar," Sir Henry assured her with a grin of such perfect camaraderie that Marianne could no longer feel even slightly discomfited by his admiration.

"I have been told very much the same thing," she laughed, and settled into a chair that was drawn up by the case that held the scroll in question.

Within a very short amount of time she had forgotten Arabella's discrete presence entirely, as well as the shortness of her acquaintance with Sir Henry and the fact that there were other guests in the house that should not be neglected for too long. Everything else seemed to fade away in her enjoyment of discussing the translation with a like-minded companion, and she quickly stopped being amazed at her own comfort in interrupting and arguing although his easy acceptance of her uninhibited contributions continued to be a pleasant novelty.

It was something of a shock to be jolted from their lively discussion sometime later by the sudden presence of Lord Willingham, who looked both aggrieved and bemused.

"If this is the thanks I am to receive for dragging that wretched crate all the way home from Greece, Marianne, I must say that you are unlikely to receive another such a present from me," he remarked with a wry smile. "Here I have been deprived of my wife's company for more than an hour, and I can assure you that Mr. Baxley is but a sad substitute."

"That would be a far lovelier compliment if I did not know perfectly well that you would consider any horse in your stables a better substitute than that man," laughed Arabella, returning from her discrete corner.

"As would any sane person," her husband retorted softly with a shudder that was not entirely in jest.

"Where is he?" Marianne whispered as if expecting him to appear at any moment.

"I left him with your father," Lord Willingham admitted. "I have spent almost the entire unending span of time trying to avoid responding to a volley of bold questions and assumptions. Upon my word, Marianne, if I did not know any better, I should think that Baxley has been your established suitor for the past year at the least. The man seems to think your engagement is a foregone conclusion."

"Your noble and heroic sacrifice is most certainly noted and appreciated," Marianne assured him solemnly. "You are a prince among brothers-in-law, quite peerless, I am sure."

"As your only brother-in-law at the moment and for the foreseeable future, I also am sure that I am quite peerless. And as such I am not above begging you to make a little more haste in discouraging Baxley for I am certain that I shall prove incapable of surviving the honor of having that gentleman as *my* brother-in-law."

"I would love to do just that, once and for all, but it is remarkably difficult to discourage a person who has made up their mind with such shocking disregard for my temperament or character or opinions," sighed Marianne. "I suspect Mr. Baxley thinks such things as the future bride's sensibilities are very minor considerations indeed, when contemplating the suitability of a match."

"But surely there is no need for you to expend any wasted effort convincing the man of anything, is there?" asked Sir Henry, who then looked rather chagrined at his boldness. "I beg your pardon. I did not intend to speak my thoughts aloud. It is of course not my place to interject in such a conversation." He looked away, embarrassed by his own forthrightness.

"We have rather moved past that, I should think, as we are having the conversation in such a way that you can scarcely be expected to escape it," Marianne laughed, the now-familiar blush rising to her cheeks once again.

"Quite so, and besides I believe I like the sound of any argument for speaking *less* to my companion of the past hour," added Lord Willingham bracingly.

"It only strikes me, as an outsider to the situation, of course, so I may easily be mistaken, that you are under no compulsion to persuade any gentleman that you would not suit him. You need only say so," Sir Henry said with a serious expression. "The burden of proof lies with him, and he should be willing to shoulder the responsibility. If he is so bold as to make a declaration without any real encouragement then you would have the opportunity of giving him whatever response pleases you, but you can hardly be held responsible for whatever illusions a man cherishes independently of reality."

Marianne blinked at Sir Henry, who gave a self-deprecating shrug as he concluded his speech, while Lord Willingham gave a heartfelt "Hear, hear."

"You are quite correct, Sir Henry, and we are indebted to your outsider's eye," declared Arabella with an approving laugh. "I believe we have been paralyzed by politeness, to some extent, and lost sight of logical thought. Of course, Marianne is under no compulsion to give Mr. Baxley anything beyond an answer to a direct question. It is not as though our father is insisting upon the match, far from it. But we really must return to the others now, I am afraid, we have tarried here far too long as it is. Have you two managed to find out whatever it is you need to know about the scroll?"

"In the space of one short hour?" Marianne gave her sister a pitying shake of the head. "Certainly not. We shall have to resume tomorrow."

"I would scarcely like to speculate on such a cursory examination," Sir Henry agreed earnestly. "Although I may venture to say that it certainly looks promising." That is, of course, certain phrases that we are using to approximate the date."

"Sir Henry, I believe that such an explanation would lead us, or some of us, at least, to continue neglecting the other guests for another hour at the very least, based on my experience with my sister," said Arabella hastily. "Come along now, both of you. We must rescue our father."

"It is a difficult assumption to argue against, unfortunately, seeing as it is perfectly accurate," Sir Henry murmured companionably to Marianne as they allowed themselves to be chivvied out of the library like a pair of wayward geese.

"And perfectly tempting, moreover," she laughed.

"But then we would be deprived of the enjoyment of working together to authenticate the scroll more fully tomorrow, so I believe I am content after all," he replied with another warm glance in her direction.

CHAPTER 18

If Marianne had resented Daphne's gleeful enjoyment of her farcical introduction to Sir Henry at the beginning of the evening, she could scarcely bring herself to feel a similar resentment at the evening's bizarre conclusion. She reflected later that perhaps it was one of those days that were simply fated to vacillate between the sublime and the ridiculous, although she had not even the presence of mind to think so at the moment.

Marianne been more or less successful in ignoring Baxley's renewed and enthusiastically blundering attentions once she rejoined their guests. She was on the point of breathing a discrete sigh of relief that the evening was drawing to a close and the guests were about to depart. Sir Henry had regretfully turned down Lord Sedgewick's invitation to take advantage of their hospitality for the remainder of his visit. He's stated he had already taken rooms at a nearby, and very comfortable, inn and would not like to disrupt the family any more than his unexpected appearance already had. Baxley had not bothered to conceal his pleasure at this development and seemed determined to keep his perceived rival for Marianne's attentions as far away as possible.

"Does Baxley *mean* to bear such a striking resemblance to a sheep dog?" Marianne heard Lord Willingham murmur whimsically to his wife. It was all she could do to quell a giggle at the idea, which once presented was impossible to banish. The older gentleman really looked like nothing so much as an energetic collie, darting and feinting both verbally and physically in his efforts to separate Marianne from her scholarly guest.

Meeting Sir Henry eyes at that moment proved more than her equanimity could bear, and Marianne found herself sharing a laugh with the gentleman that would certainly have offended Mr. Baxley had he not been distracted by the sudden appearance of yet another guest.

"Why, Captain Larkin," exclaimed Arabella, seeing that Marianne was rendered temporarily useless by the intrusion at a moment that was already so odd. "How lovely to see you this evening. We had thought that all of your party was busy with preparations for your mother's arrival. Mrs. Millworth and Ellen have talked of nothing else for several days."

"Indeed, we have been quite absorbed by just that," agreed the captain with a graceful bow. Although he spoke to Arabella, Marianne could not help but notice that his eyes remained fixed upon her own face, his expression serious and searching. "I apologize for the intrusion, but I realized that in my preoccupation I have failed to keep proper track of my ward. Elizabeth *is* here, is she not? I meant to collect her earlier this afternoon, but being the new guardian, that I am, I simply forgot the appointment. I feel quite the fool."

"Certainly, she is here, but she and Daphne have already retired for the evening," Arabella replied mildly. "I can wake her, if you wish. I believe we were under the impression that she had your consent to spend the past few days here."

"No, do not disturb her. I suppose I did say that she might. Daphne's companionship has done a great deal for her, and I am indebted for the assistance."

"I shall tell her in the morning that you called, and that you wish for her to return for a short while. We are delighted to have her, of course, but I daresay that Daphne's influence has encouraged her to forego asking permission to extend her visits here," Marianne said, finding her tongue with some difficulty, and keeping her tone as mild as Arabella's with even greater trouble. Perhaps the captain detected the barely concealed censure in her voice, for he winced slightly.

"The fault is entirely mine, Lady Marianne. I fear I have been only too willing to embrace a certain abstraction lately, taking advantage of your kindness," he said, looking sincerely chastened. "It is not a pleasant truth to realize about myself, but I have undeniably neglected my duties as the girl's guardian."

Marianne could not manage to hold on to the sharpest edge of her frustration, particularly not when she had scarcely been blameless of the same infraction. Attempting to decipher the scrolls, maintain her household obligations, and banish wayward thoughts of Captain Larkin had consumed nearly all of her thoughts for the past few weeks. She had been just as content as he to accept Elizabeth's presence as a matter of course. Besides, she could see clearly that accusing himself of neglecting his duties was a far more painful thing for a military-trained officer than it would be to an ordinary civilian.

"I hardly think that any blame needs to be apportioned, Captain," she said, temporarily putting aside what she considered to be her valid, if inexplicable, frustration that sweet, shy Elizabeth did not occupy more of the captain's time and attention. She met his eyes, breaking her own resolution to avoid doing just that, and was suddenly confused by the intense and conflicted gaze that was fixed upon her.

Her heart leapt in her chest and seemed to continue beating in her throat, thus constricting her ability to speak. Try as she might, she simply could not imagine what Captain Larkin might be thinking. Her gaze involuntarily darted back to Sir Henry. They were so very different, Captain Larkin, tall and resolute, the epitome of masculine stature, and Sir Henry, serious and bookish. She found her comparison of them troubling. Hadn't Arabella and Ellen suggested she might find a gentleman who actually liked her intellect and who might be able to share her flights of fancy? Might that person be Sir Henry?

Certainly, Sir Henry seemed to enjoy her company, and she enjoyed his. Or was it that he, like she, was so engrossed in academic endeavors that the excitement felt was not truly for each other but for the work? She was not sure, but she was certain that she did not see Sir Henry in the same light as Captain Larkin, but then, no person was seen as another. She didn't see Arabella in the same light as Daphne, and yet she cared for both. What was the difference then, she wondered, but even as she mulled the thought around in her head, she realized she liked Sir Henry, but she didn't see him as anything but an academic.

That is, she did not see him as she did Captain Larkin. Or perhaps, seeing was not the right sense at all. She was not sure she really just saw Captain Larkin. She seemed to experience him with her whole being. She was aware of him as she had never been aware of another person. Something about him touched her heart—her soul.

Just then, Mr. Baxley made an impatient noise, drawing Marianne's attention back to the rest of the assembled guests. It struck her as suddenly bizarre to see the three gentlemen standing so close together, their focus fixed unmistakably upon her. Mr. Baxley's intentions towards her were as clear as they were unwanted, but she could not quite dismiss his presence since he was continuing to jockey for a position of greater prominence.

As for Sir Henry and Captain Larkin, Marianne could not claim to *know* with any degree of certainty what they thought of her. But it was obvious both men were ignoring the existence of everyone else at that moment. They were a fascinating study in contrasts, she thought, Sir Henry's good looks being pale and refined in marked opposition to Captain Larkin's muscular, action-ready handsomeness. It seemed the height of conceit to think that both were surveying her with the same admiration, and one another with the same marked jealousy, as Mr. Baxley. Still, she could not quite dismiss the notion, any more than she could think of anything whatsoever to say. Instead, she studied the men as if they were some academic projects. Baxley , soft as dough, was immediately dismissed. Sir Henry, with the scholarly stance that would rival any of the Greek playwrights she so admired, could not be so easily set aside. He was cool and austere, not entirely unlike herself. She understood him, and liked him. He engaged her mind. But Captain Larkin was an enigma. He was everything she was not, and he had a power that was a mystery to her, a mystery she wanted to unlock. That mystery seemed to set her aflame with only a look.

It was Lord Sedgewick who mercifully broke into the surreal moment, clearing his throat and rather pointedly telling his son-in-law that he was grateful to him for sparing Arabella all afternoon.

"You know I am always happy to be of assistance, Father," said Arabella, catching ahold of the lifeline faster than her husband. "But I confess I am dreadfully tired now."

"Ah, yes, perhaps we had best be going along, then," Lord Willingham agreed hastily, shaking himself a little.

As Lord Sedgewick had obviously intended, the departure of the couple prompted the rest of the guests to take their leave as well, although each gentleman seemed to Marianne's suddenly exhausted eye very loathe to be the first to depart.

As they took their leave, she continued to evaluate the men. Mr. Baxley held her hand too long, and she would have said, too tightly, but that was not exactly right. He had a limp grip, not a tight one, but clung like stickers in the wood. She wanted to brush her gloved hand against her dress to remove the touch of him.

Sir Henry was formal and polite, just brushing his lips above her glove and promising that on the morrow, they would explore the scroll. His eyes were alight with passion, but she was not sure the passion was for her. Perhaps it was all for the scroll. Still, she could not fault him for that when she felt the same.

When Captain Larkin took her hand, the world seemed to stop. There was nothing but the sense of him before her—filling her. She unconsciously leaned in and caught the faint smell of sandalwood and leather. The scent was so intoxicating. She could feel the heat of him through her glove, his lips on the back of her hand and even the trace of a callous as they stood palm to palm with only the fine fabric of her glove separating them. No doubt his hands were hardened from the reins of a horse, held, checked and pushed to the limit in his capable hands, a ride of life and death. It was impossible to feel all of that in the brief touch, and yet she did, and more.

She felt the blushing warmth on her face suffuse through her with unquenchable heat, and she moistened her lips as if to satiate some unknown thirst. The captain smiled his half smile as if he knew something she didn't, something she desperately wanted to learn, but he only took his leave, and she felt the loss of him. She folded her arms over her bosom as if to warm herself.

When they had all finally gone, Marianne sucked in a slow breath and hesitantly looked up at her father, who was frowning at the door with his heavy eyebrows lowered.

"Really, my dear, *three* admirers at the same dinner party seems rather excessive I should think. You must try to space them out a little better in the future, or else we shall be in danger of guests who never leave for fear of giving up some imagined advantage," he said at length, giving her a kiss on the cheek and striding away without giving her a chance to respond.

"I didn't actually invite any of them," Marianne felt compelled to point out, although she could not tell if her father heard her or not. It was foolish and shallow, she knew, but she could not help feeling a little elated that he seemed confident in classifying all three gentlemen as her admirers, and despite her exhaustion and profound confusion, she smiled at the idea all the way up to her chamber.

CHAPTER 19

Marianne's confused pleasure did not linger as long as she might have hoped, being mitigated by a night of interrupted sleep. First, she tossed and dreamed and then Elizabeth's cries woke her. Added to that, she found that her hopes regarding the authenticity of the scroll had been raised almost unbearably by Sir Henry's cautious initial assessment, and she could scarcely stand the strain of waiting longer for a final decision, no matter how she might scold Daphne on the necessity of patience and painstaking methodologies.

When Captain Larkin arrived at midday to collect Elizabeth, Marianne was automatically annoyed to be pulled away from the library where she had been doing her best to remain calm and scholarly. In fact, she had gone so far as to retrieve some needlework to keep herself from hovering over Sir Henry as he worked, but that did not stop her from asking so many questions that she was sure Sir Henry was becoming perturbed. She forced herself to sit near the maid who had joined her for propriety's sake.

Marianne took the moment to concentrate on her needlework although the scroll was foremost in her mind. She itched to stand at Sir Henry's shoulder. She realized that unlike her wish to be near Captain Larkin, her wish to be near Sir Henry was primarily due to the academic nature of the scroll rather than the man himself.

Where had that thought come from? She had resolved that she put all thoughts of Captain Larkin from her mind, and yet there he was at the forefront once again. Her temper was not improved by the realization that the morning had passed by entirely before he could be bothered to attend to his ward who was still above stairs with Daphne getting into who knew what trouble.

"Lady Marianne, I hope you are well?" the captain asked when she emerged reluctantly from the library and directed a maid to bring a pot of tea. She sent a footman to locate the girls, who could be anywhere in the rather large house.

Marianne's hand went to her hair, which she undoubtedly had mussed while studying the scroll. Captain Larkin's look of scrutiny was not altogether flattering, and Marianne recalled the dark circles rather prominently featured in her looking-glass reflection when she arose that morning. Annoyance at appearing less than beautiful in his presence, and perhaps even sharper annoyance at herself for entertaining such a foolish notion that he cared if she was beautiful or not, made her forget to temper her words with patience.

"I am well enough, sir, only tired from having my sleep disrupted yet again," she retorted tartly, "and Sir Henry wanted to get an early start on the scroll. Of course, you are well-acquainted with poor Elizabeth's nightmares, I suppose? She was visited by a particularly upsetting one several times over the course of the night, and although I do not begrudge her any amount of my sleep, it would be inaccurate to claim that I am not feeling the lack of it today. Ah, there is our tea," she said as the maid brought in the pot.

"Elizabeth's...nightmares?" the captain looked at once bewildered and chastened. Just as Marianne had suspected, he had known of no such thing, and she took an uncharitable relish at his discomfiture. It proved that he was not the paragon she had made up in her musings. He was indeed human, and the thought brought her back to earth.

"Yes, certainly. She is prone to waking with them at least once in the night; several times if she has been overtired or excited during the day. Occasionally they are interspersed with episodes of walking in her sleep. Surely, you had observed this?" Marianne spoke as she poured the tea.

The maid, aware of the impropriety of receiving a gentleman without a chaperone present, busied herself with darning socks in a corner of the morning room while Marianne and the captain had tea. Marianne was sure that Daphne and Elizabeth would join them momentarily. The footman had only to find them.

"I must confess in all honesty that I have not observed any such thing, Lady Marianne, which is hardly to my credit," said the captain. "I left here last evening feeling that I was guilty of neglecting my duty towards my ward and towards her father who entrusted her care to me. I see now that I had not even begun to comprehend the extent of my neglect. It only compounds my shame that you have been burdened and wearied."

Captain Larkin looked so contrite, and so disgusted with himself, that Marianne felt a flush for her own short temper. She was certainly being rude, and she made an effort to correct her manners.

"Elizabeth could never be a burden, Captain Larkin, and I fear that I must apologize to you for speaking so shrewishly just now," she said with a weary sigh, taking a seat as the sudden ebb and flow of emotions left her feeling nearly as exhausted as she looked. "It has done Daphne nearly as much good to have such a dear companion as it has done Elizabeth, I daresay. I would be a cold-hearted monster indeed to prize a little sleep over the comfort and well-being of a child. I have been just as guilty as yourself in being preoccupied with my own thoughts and allowing the girls to do as they pleased these past few weeks, so really, I have no right to make you feel badly over the same fault."

"I daresay that you have every right, Lady Marianne, but of course I do not think that was your intention," he replied, taking a seat across from her, and meeting her gaze with such a steady concern that she felt quite vexed with herself.

"It certainly *was* my intention," she admitted bluntly, making him widen his eyes in surprise at her candor. "I was feeling nettled and cross, for any number of reasons, and I felt quite gleeful at the opportunity to prove to you so neatly that you have not been giving the child the attention I think she deserves. It was hideously unkind of me, to say nothing of it being it is none of my business. The only excuse I can claim is that I *am* dreadfully tired today." She took a large sip of tea to fortify herself. "But I do apologize, sir, if it makes any difference to you."

"Truly, Lady Marianne, you are a remarkably unusual creature," he said after studying her for a long moment. "There are very few people, at least of my own acquaintance, and I have encountered many individuals in my travels, who would be so straightforward in acknowledging and apologizing for such a thing. Or indeed, for any number of far more egregious deeds than the dubious crime of being impatient with a fool."

"I am aware that my way of speaking is far too forthright and direct to conform to the accepted standards for ladylike comportment, but I fear I cannot see any use in permitting self-deception, or really most forms of prevarication. What virtue is served by pretending that I have been motivated by better intentions than I really was? It is hard enough to know the truth in general, without further muddying the waters for the sake of a little polite comfort."

"I said that there are very few *people* of my acquaintance who would speak in such a manner. I said nothing of ladies. Indeed, my life has been such that I encounter ladies and polite society a great deal less than most. I am far more familiar with the habits of brave and hardened soldiers, and I can assure you that the vast majority of them would still shy away from preventing someone from providing them with an excuse. I am speaking of valor, not ladylike or unladylike conduct, or any manner of gentile comportment.

"Oh," Marianne said, rather pointlessly, feeling entirely unsure of her footing all of the sudden. "You are right, that *is* what you said, and I leaped to my own conclusions based, in all likelihood, on the fact that the incompatibility of my femininity and my mind has been brought to the forefront a great deal lately."

"You certainly must be quite weary, then, since I have never known you to misunderstand anything," the captain said in a gently teasing tone. "Particularly not a matter regarding precision of language. Indeed, you did not even correct me when I termed you a remarkably unusual creature, and I heard the redundancy of that description even as I was employing it."

"I *did* notice that, but I do attempt to refrain from correcting such things. People find it annoying, you know, and besides I did not think it fair to mention after pointing out so many other mistakes you have made," she retorted with an answering smile of her own as she eyed him over her cup.

He laughed aloud at that, and Marianne was gratified to know that he recognized her teasing and did not take offense.

"And those mistakes are a great deal more important, which I suppose is why I keep distracting myself from thinking of them," Captain Larkin sighed, the momentary merriment fading from his manner almost at once. "It is certainly unpleasant to think how disappointed my friend would be if he could see just how misguided he had been to trust the care of his child with such a self-absorbed fool."

"That is entirely too harsh a judgement," argued Marianne, who could not keep her heart from going out to the plain misery on his face. She sat her teacup in its saucer with a clink. "It is not as though any harm has come to Elizabeth while you have been lost in abstraction."

"A very kind way of saying it, Lady Marianne, but the truth of the matter is that I have been less lost in abstraction and more stubbornly brooding. There seems to have been a great cloud over me and I have not even attempted to shake free of the thing. I am not made for a steady sort of civilian life, and this extended stay would doubtless be wearing on me even without my grief at the death of my dearest friend and my frustration over choosing my next post."

"*That* is what has been bothering me so much about this situation." Marianne exclaimed, startling the captain.

CHAPTER 20

"I beg your pardon; I did not mean to sound so unfeeling just as you were speaking of your grief," she added rather sheepishly, realizing that she had made her outburst without any thought as to the gravity of what Captain Larkin had been saying.

"No, no, a burst of clarity comes when it will," he laughed. "What was your revelation?"

"Only that I have been rather mystified by the personal sort of frustration that I have felt anytime I contemplate your, forgive me, your cavalier manner of approaching the responsibilities of guardianship. It bothers me unendingly to be unable to identify the underlying reason or cause of my own emotions, even more so in this case, with Arabella and Ellen suggesting that it was perhaps due to my feelings of—" Marianne broke off suddenly, heat suffusing her face, for in her enthusiasm she had been about to unintentionally admit that her closest companions suspected she harbored feelings of admiration and affection for the captain.

"Yes?" he inquired in a mildly prompting tone, kindly pretending not to see her blush and confusion. His lips quirked in the smallest of smiles, slightly pursed with amusement. They were full and well-formed—quite nice lips, she thought.

She suddenly wondered what those lips would feel like against her own. Would they have the firm control hinted at by his calloused hands? A shiver went through her from the dryness of her own lips to settle somewhere in her midsection and lower where a sudden heat pooled. Marianne shook herself from the musings with a gasp of horror at the licentious turn her thoughts had taken. Her eyes strayed briefly to the maid seated unobtrusively in the corner and wondered where Daphne and Elizabeth were.

"It has bothered me," she said, redirecting the stream of her words and speaking in a more subdued manner. "And I have just realized that the reason for that is quite personal and specific. It is perhaps also why Daphne and Elizabeth have found it easy to become such close friends so quickly. You know, of course, that our mother died when Daphne was quite young. Arabella and I were not even half grown ourselves, but Father became so mired in grief that he could scarcely attend to our upbringing. I do not say this to blame him, of course. He loved our mother very much and her loss was simply more than he could bear. By the time his grief became somewhat bearable we had all settled into habits and roles that made it simple for him to remain very remote."

"And you do not want Elizabeth to experience the same sort of distant caregiver, knowing from firsthand experience that it is far from ideal," Captain Larkin nodded, inhaling deeply as he contemplated her words. "That does make perfect sense."

"The situations are nothing like perfect parallels, however, and I feel I must apologize for casting yourself and Elizabeth in those roles. I fear I am not myself today." Between the lack of sleep and the concern over the scroll and the consternation over her feelings for Sir Henry and Captain Larkin, she was seriously vexed with herself. She usually was in much more control of herself.

"You must apologize for nothing," he corrected, not sharply, but firmly. "It is a sensitive and empathetic spirit that can identify such similarities and feel so strongly. And I must be allowed to express my sincere gratitude that you have made the connection. Both Elizabeth and I may benefit from the wisdom and insight that you have gained from your experience."

"I fear my wisdom and insight are in rather short supply just now, but you are welcome to the small portion that I *do* feel certain of. A child knows instinctively, I think, when they are a secondary consideration to the person who is in charge of them. I daresay that is an unpleasant sensation for any person, but different temperaments respond to it in their own ways. For example, my older sister took it upon herself to take such perfect care of us all that Father never need be bothered by anything."

"Rather, a tall order for a child," Captain Larkin commented. "Although from what I have learned of your sister during my visit, I imagine she tolerated nothing less than success."

"Precisely so," agreed Marianne with a bittersweet smile. "She especially strove to keep us all so far from any whiff of danger or scandal or even unhappiness that she eventually became almost dangerously selfless. We all allowed, and I suppose even tacitly encouraged, Arabella to embrace such an impossible role that she very nearly forgot that her own happiness was a thing worthy of any consideration at all. And Daphne, of course, responded to our father's preoccupation by becoming as wild and willful as she possibly could in order to garner his notice. Really, Captain Larkin, neither response is something that anyone who cares for Elizabeth would choose for her."

"No, it is not," he mused. "But you have left one sister out of your cautionary tale. How did you respond, Lady Marianne?"

"I? I believe it was by escaping as much as possible into books and study. Arabella indulged me, of course, and left me to wallow in the library as much as I wanted without being burdened with so many of the adult cares that she had taken upon herself. I was always happiest there, able to put aside problems that have no solution, for those that could be resolved by the end of the chapter. Doubtless I would have done much the same thing regardless of my father's involvement and attention, but perhaps not to such an exclusive degree that I am now so ill-suited for my role. Not that I blame him, of course," she added hastily. "Or Arabella either. Everyone did the best they could at the moment, I believe, and my social inadequacy is ultimately no one's fault but my own."

"I have yet to witness any social inadequacy, Lady Marianne. If I thought that the only side effect of continuing my selfish abstraction would be to mold Elizabeth into such an intelligent and well-educated person as yourself, I admit I would be tempted to change very little as regards to my approach. However, it seems you have been unhappy, and are perhaps unhappy still, and I would not wish that for my ward at any price."

"No, of course not," Marianne murmured, struck by her companion's choice of words. *Was* she unhappy? Had she been unhappy prior to Arabella's marriage, when she had been able to study to her heart's content? Was the enjoyable escape of books not quite the complete replacement of positive interactions that she had always thought?

"What is it that you are thinking?" wondered Captain Larkin, and Marianne could not help but note that his tone hit the perfect note, prompting her notice without demanding it, not impatient for her to resume conversation but curious as to what might be taking place in her mind. It was a small thing, yet so rare as to be exceedingly valuable to her.

"I was remembering that I used to have bad dreams as a child as well, and wondering if perhaps my ploy of avoiding the emotions of a less-than-ideal reality might have resulted in those emotions surfacing in sleep," she replied slowly, frowning a little in concentration. "It is rather like principles of mathematics and physics; equations must be balanced, pressure unreleased must find a vent."

"Like water that has been dammed up?" he suggested.

"Something along those lines, yes. My knowledge of the proper construction of dams is rather limited, although I mean to change that presently."

He raised an eyebrow, but she continued without a breath, not explaining that she often pursued learning for learning's sake without any real need for the knowledge. "I should imagine that if the water builds up too much and is not allowed some alternate path, it presses through the dam itself."

"I believe that is so, and moreover I believe that within six weeks' time you will know more about the proper construction of dams and any number of other such things than most of Britain's finest engineers," said the captain with a look of amusement mixed with admiration. "I must say, I am rather in awe of your mind, Lady Marianne, and its ability to leap with such agility from one topic to the next, linking things that seem entirely dissimilar to me, such as thoughts and feelings with equations and mechanics."

The admiration was so evident on his face that Marianne could not doubt it, nor could she detect any trace of the tiresome masculine discomfort that so often accompanied the realization of her intellect. She started to ask a question that had been nagging at her ever since Captain

Larkin had arrived in their village, but her courage failed her at the last instant. Telling herself it was a matter of focus rather than cowardice; she gave a little sigh and replied to him instead.

"Do not be too impressed, sir, for it is hardly an original thought of mine. Descartes discussed such things more than a hundred years previously."

"How foolish of me to have forgotten about Descartes," the captain said wryly, "My only excuse in neglecting to give him credit is that neither he, nor my tutor were charming enough instructors to hold my attention as you do, Lady Marianne."

His marked flirtation was so decidedly, and excitingly, appealing that Marianne hastily redirected the conversation once again. That gallant charm of his was more than likely unintentional, and she could easily imagine that he had unwittingly left a trail of broken hearts behind him at every port. She did not intend to join that company. It was clear he was not marriage minded.

"But do you know, I think that my own bad dreams as a child were of a rather different type than Elizabeth's nightmares. Perhaps it is only due to the innumerable differences between one mind and the next, but I somehow doubt it."

"Different in what ways?"

"Well, I never woke up actually screaming in fright or walked in my sleep as far as I am aware. But more than that even, my bad dreams were always an unsettling and disordered sort of jumble. I do not recall that the same person or event was ever present more than once, yet Elizabeth dreams almost the same thing every time, or at least, every time she has a terrible night."

Captain Larkin lay aside his napkin and leaned forward. "I have known fellow soldiers to be haunted by the same dream, or variations of it, after a particularly vicious battle," mused Captain Larkin. "For some it passes away within a few weeks or months, but I have known others that seem to sink beneath the weight of it even in their waking moments, to never truly recover the well-being they previously possessed. I think perhaps it would be a good idea to speak with Roger on this matter. He has examined her, and I know he feels her physical health is improving nicely, but I would feel better all the same to have a physician's opinion, and my brother would be the one I would most trust."

"I think you are right. Really, I ought to have thought of it myself ages ago," Marianne resisted the unreasonable impulse to squirm with guilt at the realization.

"It was not your responsibility to think of it," the captain said gently.

"Nonetheless, from everything I have read on the matter lately, it seems there is an inextricable link between the health of the mind and the health of the body. It may be unreasonable to hope that Doctor Larkin can prescribe the exact tonic that will eradicate all dreams of short balding men with red eyebrows and burn marks on their hands, but I am confident that he can do *something* to help ease Elizabeth's sleep."

"What did you say?" demanded Captain Larkin in a voice so sharp and full of tension that Marianne blinked at him as if she had never seen him before in her life. Indeed, he seemed to have been replaced by a dangerous stranger, one ready for violence and action without a moment's notice, before her very eyes.

"I did not mean to disparage your brother's skill as a physician," she said with cautious confusion. "I have the greatest faith in his abilities. We have always said that we are fortunate indeed to have him-"

"Not about Roger," he cut her off impatiently. "About the bald man. Red eyebrows and burn marks on his hands, you said? That seems very specific for a dream."

"Yes, I thought so too, but often dreams will create something odd. In any case, that is how Elizabeth always describes him. He seems to be the principal antagonist in her nightmares, I do not think she has yet to recount one where he was absent. But why should that matter so particularly to you?"

"Because," the captain said in such a grim voice that it sent chills down Marianne's spine. "That is the exact description of one of the most dangerous and notorious spies in all of Europe."

CHAPTER 21

Whatever Marianne had expected Captain Larkin to say, it had most decidedly not been that. For a moment all she could manage to do was to stare blankly at him.

"You think he is real?" She blurted at last.

"I most certainly hope not, but what other notion would elicit such nightmares?"

Marianne shook her head. "But I have asked Elizabeth if she had ever met that person in real life, and she seemed quite certain that she had not," she protested rather lamely once she found her voice.

"I daresay that either you or my brother will have some scientific or philosophical explanation for a child forgetting an unpleasant memory only to have it resurface in dreams, or *not* forgetting entirely, but being unwilling to relate the memory aloud." He stood as if he could not sit idly by now that there was a focus to his ward's nightmare. He paced away from the table and then turned back to her. "But what are the odds that the daughter of an officer is visited by recurring dreams that feature a villain of *la Fumèe*'s exact description without ever having encountered the man?" he asked with pardonable impatience.

"Statistically unlikely," Marianne murmured, mentally ordering herself to refrain from launching into the series of calculations needed to answer a question that was clearly rhetorical. "The spy is called *la Fumèe*? The smoke?"

"No one has discovered the man's true identity," Captain Larkin explained, looking as though this fact was a personal affront. "Most known spies are given such foolish titles, for want of something to call them, I suppose. In this case it is more accurate than fanciful for once, for *la Fumèe* is quite as impossible to catch as smoke. Added to which he seems to have a particular affinity for choking his victims. A nice, silent, bloodless way to remove an obstacle."

Marianne blanched. "He sounds more like an assassin than a spy," she objected, for the sake of having *something* to say.

"I am sorry. I misspoke. I should not have been so descriptive to a lady." He came back to the table and took her hand in a comforting gesture. The gesture, was anything but comforting. She was not wearing gloves. It was the first time that he had touched her, skin to skin and it was a heady experience indeed. A fire seemed to leap between them and the racing of her heart had nothing to do with the assassin and everything to do with the handsome man in front of her.

Marianne shook her head negating his caution and bringing her thoughts back to the present problem. "No. If we are to help Elizabeth, I should know about this man."

"Most spies – and assassins, too, for that matter – are not overly particular about that distinction. *La Fumèe* may not go out of his way to kill, or to secure work specifically as an assassin, but he certainly does not quibble about removing any obstacles to his primary goal. In fact, a certain dogged, relentless determination to reach his objective is one of *la Fumèe's* distinguishing characteristics. Those burn marks on his hands? They are from retrieving certain important documents from a fire. You can well imagine that no spy would care to voluntarily receive such memorable and difficult to hide features; yet he prized his goal over even his anonymity."

"And you think that Elizabeth has encountered this man somehow?" Marianne shuddered at the thought, unable to shake the chill that her companion's grim description had elicited. "If that is the case, then small wonder the poor child has been having nightmares."

"I must ask her to be certain," the captain said.

"Yes, of course," Marianne said. "I'm sure the girls were busy with some project or they would have come to tea by now."

"It is no matter," Captain Larkin said with a frown. "In any case, I fear that an interrogation into such a sensitive subject may upset her further and perhaps cause harm. With your permission, I will go fetch my brother before speaking to her. His presence is soothing in a general sort of way, and I would prefer to rely on the wisdom of his expertise in this matter."

"Of course, that is no trouble. I told the girls that you would be coming to collect Elizabeth this morning, which I daresay has had the direct result of encouraging them to spend their time somewhere as remote and inconvenient as possible in order to delay their parting. If I start hunting them down now, I *may* just locate them by the time you return."

"I fear I am causing you further inconvenience, right on the heels of my apology which I assure you was most sincere and heartfelt. I ought to retrieve Elizabeth now and have Roger speak to her at his home, to avoid keeping you from your guest any further, but I suspect that Elizabeth will be more at ease in this environment. Would you mind very much?"

"Of course not. Do not worry on that account," Marianne laughed with a fond glance in the direction of the library. She had completely forgotten about the man, and obviously Sir Henry had forgotten her as well engrossed in the scroll as he was.

"Sir Henry is entirely absorbed in the process of authentication just now, and I have no doubt that he is lost to the world for some hours longer unless he is dragged into the present by force. And besides, surely Doctor Larkin will need to hear my own description of Elizabeth's nightmares and sleepwalking firsthand. Do bring him here."

"Lady Marianne, you are the most fascinating individual," the captain stated taking her hand in his without seeming to notice that he was doing so. Marianne could feel her pulse quicken involuntarily at the simple contact. How was it that this man could affect her so with only a touch?

"That is a statement that might be interpreted any number of ways, and not all of them particularly complimentary," she returned, making her comment as light and careless as possible, but she feared there was a tremor in her voice.

"You may choose whichever interpretation you like and it would be accurate enough," he answered paradoxically, rising and bowing. "I shall return with Roger as soon as I possibly can."

MAKING HASTE TO HIS BROTHER'S HOUSE, CAPTAIN Larkin sincerely hoped he would find Roger at home. He had learned in the past few weeks that the routine of a country doctor was anything but predictable most days. Captain Larkin set his mind to recalling every scrap of information he had ever learned about *la Fumèe*, and every time he had discussed the spy with Southampton. Here was the sense of urgency, of action and possible danger that he had been missing during this tedious lull, and yet he would not put his charge in danger. How could she have met the spy? It was ludicrous. Added to that, his mind continued to return with stubborn frequency to the charming conundrum that was Lady Marianne.

As much as he valued candor and transparency, he had not quite been able to bring himself to tell her one rather large factor in his avoidance of the Sedgewick home, and by association, Elizabeth. The reasons he had given her were all true enough; his grief for his friend *had* weighed upon him terribly, as had inaction and a growing sense of dissatisfaction with his future prospects. In his mind, and hers as well, he had no doubt, those reasons were fairly valid, but scarcely compelling enough to excuse outright dereliction of duty for his ward. So, he had seen no point in mentioning an additional reason which was entirely without validity or excuse, that the continuous battle to steel himself against the impact of her allure was proving impossible to wage.

Perhaps impossible was not an entirely accurate term, he conceded, the rhythmic cadence of his boots hitting the ground with purpose and speed providing him with a steady backdrop for his thoughts. It was not *impossible* to resist even the most fascinating charms. It would be more honest to admit to himself that he was simply losing the desire to resist being fascinated. Her intelligence, her beauty, those things he might have been content to admire from afar even combined in one person as they were. His mistake had been in discovering her character as well. A mistake that had revealed, a devastating combination of sympathetic kindness, brutal honesty, and straightforward speaking. He could hardly be expected keep a steady resolve in the face of such a noble heart.

And that was without counting all the dozens of smaller characteristics and mannerisms that he found so charming. Then there was her unbridled delight and enthusiasm in learning something new or sharing her knowledge, and the rapid yet meandering stream of her thoughts when she forgot to keep them in check for the sake of others. He could listen to that all day, understanding perhaps only a mere fraction of what she said, but content to let her words flow over him like the cascade of a sparkling waterfall, but there were things he could teach her too, and she would make an eager student. He was sure of it. The thought of teaching her about love and love-making brought a rush of desire to his body, but what he wanted from her was so much more than physical.

When a man could sincerely make such a claim, he mused, there was no longer any point in pretending to himself that he was not hopelessly in love. The realization was enough to stop him dead in his tracks for a moment, just as he reached the gate to Roger's front garden. It was hardly a surprise, but it stole his breath all the same. He was in love with Lady Marianne Sedgewick, yet none of his reasons for refraining from marriage had changed. Moreover, she was unlikely to have him, regardless. She could never be happy with a simple soldier like himself, a man unable to reference long-dead Greek and French philosophers or innovative modern scientists in casual everyday conversation. She ought to be with someone who could at least approach her level of intellectual brilliance, someone like that wretched Sir Henry Downing who had apparently materialized for the sole purpose of showing him just how inadequate a suitor he was.

He had seen the way the academic looked at Marianne the previous evening and had no doubt the man desired her. Andrew could hardly fault him for his good taste, but it had been galling to realize that if Marianne had been forced to rank the gentlemen in terms of desirability and suitability, he himself would be more on a level with foolishly self-assured Mr. Baxley than the well-read scholar. She would want a man who could talk to her for heaven's sake. He knew he was not that man, not that he wanted to simply talk. He wanted to take her in his arms and kiss her senseless. He wanted to see the wonder in her eyes when she embarked on this brand-new adventure, and mostly, he wanted her to look at him like she looked at that damned scroll.

"Andrew? What on earth are you standing there scowling at those poor holly bushes for? I thought you were going to fetch Elizabeth."

Ellen's sweet, laughing voice broke into his thoughts, and he realized that he certainly had been regarding the freshly trimmed holly with a ferocious scowl, his fists clenched wrathfully.

"I was just thinking of something particularly unpleasant," he replied, forcing his expression into a sheepish smile for the benefit of his future sister-in-law. "It seems to be my season for such things."

"Things *do* seem to go in seasons like that," she agreed sympathetically. "But the wheel always turns around again, doesn't it?"

"In general, although I do not entirely see how that is possible in this case."

"Which is just what one feels right before everything improves, so really you may look at that as a very good sign. But where is Elizabeth?"

"Still at the Sedgewick's estate. I came back to fetch Roger so he can help me question her about a matter I fear will be very distressing for the child," he answered, feeling both disingenuous and self-centered, for Ellen would certainly attribute his bleak mood to concern over his ward's well-being rather than wounded pride and lovesickness. "Do you know if Roger is home?"

"He is here. We have only just returned from visiting our favorite little recovering invalid," she replied with a fond smile at the thought of the ailing little boy whose family lived on a small nearby farm, who was so much stronger and livelier than he had been earlier in the year. "He is seeing a patient who was here waiting for him when we got back, so I have been keeping out of the way by inspecting all the architect's progress. It is coming along marvelously, don't you think? But Roger ought to be finished quite soon and will be free to go with you. Is Elizabeth unwell?"

"I am not entirely sure how to answer that, but I believe that her physical health continues to improve," he hedged cautiously, but he appreciated her concern and her uncomplicated support. "Come with me so I can explain the whole matter to you and Roger both at once."

The answer evidently pleased Ellen, whose pretty face lit up at his tacit acceptance of her as an extension of his brother. Andrew did not think there was any reason to point out that between Roger and the Sedgewick sisters it would have been senseless to try and keep any information from her even if he didn't approve of her thoroughly as a match for his favorite sibling. Fortunately, he *did*. In addition to liking her for her own sake, and since she had saved Roger's life, he could not imagine denying Ellen any request.

It was on the tip of his tongue to ask her something, he did not know entirely what. Something about Lady Marianne. Perhaps he was just looking for her assurance, but at that moment the front door opened, and Roger's patient began a slow descent of the steps. It was all for the best, he told himself, to be saved from the momentary and mad impulse to confide his foolish affections to Ellen and burden her with the knowledge of them with no real purpose. Besides, there were certainly more urgent matters at hand, and he had the sense to be grateful for the distraction.

CHAPTER 22

Marianne had only barely managed to locate the two younger girls, predictably tucked away in the most remote and seldom used garret of the estate, and chivy them into clean frocks and down the stairs before Captain Larkin returned. They were still in a rather disheveled state in spite of the change of wardrobe, and Marianne was distracted by the smudges of dust she kept noticing.

"Really, the pair of you could hardly have gotten filthier if you had rolled around in the barnyard," she scolded, feeling uncharacteristically cross. The knowledge that her heightened emotions had nothing to do with the two besmirched faces looking reproachfully into her own did nothing to alleviate her tension.

"It is far too cold for rolling around outdoors," Daphne pointed out with an absurd amount of dignity. "And besides, we wanted to search for hidden documents. You never know what sort of thing you might find tucked away by our ancestors."

"The only thing you're likely to find in that garret is dust…perhaps some mouse droppings."

"Eww," Daphne exclaimed wrinkling her nose.

"Then perhaps you should confine yourself to the part of the house that is cleaned. No one has used that part of the house even as storage for generations, and no one ever has any reason to go there. Pray do not pretend that your real purpose was anything other than making yourselves as difficult to locate as possible. I told you *specifically* that Captain Larkin would be collecting Elizabeth this morning, and that you were to stay close by."

"I am sorry, Lady Marianne," Elizabeth murmured, looking so contrite and sorrowful that Marianne's conscience instantly smote her.

"I was not scolding you, dear, I am certain that this plan was none of your doing and all of Daphne's."

"That is entirely accurate," Daphne said quickly, without the slightest hint of apology in her tone. "But you are wrong about the garret, you know, Marianne. *Someone* goes there still, for we found footprints tracked in the dust on the floor."

"If it makes you feel better to prove me wrong about something, by all means fasten onto *that* point," scoffed Marianne while taking her handkerchief none too gently to Daphne's grime-streaked cheek. "I daresay you cannot find anything more relevant to argue about anyhow."

Daphne was saved from the combined indignity of a scolding and scrubbing by the arrival of Captain Larkin, Doctor Larkin, and Ellen, who all looked grave and serious enough to quell whatever protest she had been about to make.

"Andrew has been explaining the situation to us on the walk over here," Ellen said after greetings were briefly exchanged. "I hope you do not mind that I came along, Marianne, but I thought I might be of some assistance. Perhaps Daphne and I could speak with one another in a different room? It occurred to me that she may have observed some relevant things without knowing."

"You are always welcome here, you surely know that," Marianne replied with a look of fervent gratitude. "And you are more than welcome to take Daphne out of the way just now, by all means."

"Explained all of what situation? What is going on?" demanded Daphne indignantly. She pulled away from Ellen's hand. "I will not be relegated *out of the way*," she protested.

"I will tell you all that I can. Just come with me now, dear," said Ellen. Her tone was cajoling and persuasive, but it was her firm grip on Daphne's arm that propelled the girl out of the room. Marianne allowed herself to draw a small breath of relief once the door closed behind the pair, for it was all but impossible to focus properly on the withdrawn Elizabeth as long as Daphne's more exuberant spirit was present.

"Is something wrong? Am I in trouble?" asked Elizabeth, her large eyes darting from one adult to the next in alarm, before fastening onto Marianne rather desperately. Marianne understood she was the person most familiar to Elizabeth, and it only made sense that the child would look to her in a moment of distress, but Marianne felt completely out of her depth as the child's protector.

"You have done nothing wrong, dear," she said soothingly, taking a seat beside Elizabeth and holding her hand out in encouragement. Elizabeth grasped ahold of the proffered hand promptly and clung to it like a limpet. "You aren't in any trouble. We are only a little worried about your health, and I happened to mention your troubles with unpleasant dreams to Captain Larkin."

"I am terribly sorry to cause such a disturbance, truly I am," the girl murmured, her face flushing. "Indeed, I do not ever mean to make a sound all night long. I tell myself to keep quiet, over and over as I am falling asleep, and yet I wake up already shrieking before I know what is happening."

"You are hardly to blame for that. Not even the most hardened soldier has complete control over himself in slumber," pointed out Captain Larkin with an encouraging smile.

"And certainly, I do not blame you, or think you cry out on purpose," Marianne added. "But you are not entirely strong and well yet, you know, and restful slumber is a necessary element for your health."

"Lady Marianne is quite right," agreed Doctor Larkin, his voice somehow managing to be both serious and reassuring at once. Not for the first time, Marianne marveled at his extraordinarily effective manner with his patients. It was so unusual for a man of his brilliance to also be patient and gentle. Marianne had often reflected that she could not imagine ever matching his talent in the latter area, not that she had any aspirations to be a physician.

"I feel much better than I did when I first came here," hedged Elizabeth, looking as though she might be accused of ingratitude if she admitted to feeling less than perfectly healthy.

"And you look a great deal healthier as well. Not nearly so pale or thin, and I believe that some of Daphne's vim and vigor must be transferring itself to you by dint of constant companionship," said Captain Larkin with a lightning-fast grin.

How was it his grin seemed to strike into the very heart of her, Marianne wondered, feeling her breath quicken as he addressed his ward? Marianne's fingers twitched with the need to reach out and cup his face in her hands. She noticed that a shadow appeared on his jaw and she considered how the rough stubble would feel under her fingertips, but she restrained herself as the man spoke. She forced herself to attend.

"But I imagine that you still have a way to go, Elizabeth, before you are once more as rosy and strong as we might hope," the captain said. "Why don't you tell me and Roger about the nightmare that has been troubling you, so that we may understand a little better. Lady Marianne says that you always dream of the same thing, is that correct?"

"Yes, that is true," Elizabeth agreed reluctantly, cutting her eyes to Marianne for a brief instant. "At least, I always dream of the same person, and he frightens me terribly. The rest of the dream is not always the same. I mean, different things happen, but he is always there, and I am very afraid of him."

"What does he look like, this man?" prompted Doctor Larkin gently. "Some sort of ogre or monster, perhaps?"

"No, he is an ordinary enough man. At first, he doesn't seem imposing at all. Short, with a bald head and reddish eyebrows. And there are scars--burn marks on his hands." The little girl gave an involuntary shudder at her own description of the nightmare man, as though speaking the words might conjure him into being. "His voice is very soft," she added suddenly. "But it is more frightening than if he were shouting at me."

"What is it that he says?"

"He says... he says that it is no use trying to run or hide. That no one has evaded him yet, and that a scrap of a girl-child like me is not likely to succeed where so many others have failed. He wants something, wants it badly. He seems to think I have it, but I never understand what it is or how I might give it to him. Indeed, I would gladly give him anything if it would make him stop pursuing me. In my dreams he is always following me no matter where I go or how much haste I try to make."

"Does the man ever catch you, in your dreams?" asked the captain, with a cautious glance at his brother to be certain that the question was acceptable. He was clearly out of his element, and Marianne could not help but appreciate the way he deferred to the expertise of others even though he was the sort of man who was surely used to being in command of most situations.

"No, I awake right as he is about to overtake me."

"Is the man someone you have ever met before in real life? Perhaps someone your father knew?" Doctor Larkin questioned. The guilty look that flashed over the little girl's face told the answer far more plainly than words, but she shook her head briefly before burying her face in her hands.

"I know you told me before that he was no one you had ever seen before," Marianne murmured, running a soothing hand over Elizabeth's disordered hair. "You mustn't think that I would be cross with you if you give a different answer now. There is a great deal of difference between saying something that is not strictly true in order to put an end to a distressing conversation and deliberately lying to a physician who is attempting to aid in your recovery, you know."

"Truly? But it was wrong of me to lie to you, especially when you have been so kind to me. Daphne says that falsehoods are strictly for cowards and knaves, and I suppose that is so, for I am both," sobbed Elizabeth in the most pitifully heart-rending tones imaginable.

"It *is* wrong to lie," Captain Larkin said before Marianne could think of the best way to respond to Elizabeth's distress. "And certainly, it would have been better if you had told the truth, or simply said that you did not want to speak of the matter, but you hardly qualify as coward or knave. Speaking of things that frighten us can be difficult for even the bravest and best people, you know. I suspect you will feel all the better for saying the thing aloud. Please trust me on this." He paused taking a deep breath and asked with a soft, but determined voice, "Did your father know this man?"

"Yes," Elizabeth whispered, going suddenly pale and clenching Marianne's hand painfully. "I never saw him until perhaps the last six months that Papa was alive, after we had already given up our home and began staying at the inn. Father had wanted to send me to you then. He said he would not last the winter, but I didn't want to leave him."

She suppressed a sob.

"Of course, you didn't," said Doctor Larkin sympathetically.

"He was dying," she whispered. "He did not like to speak of it. He thought I didn't know, but I knew he was dying."

"What about the man in your dreams?" Captain Larkin urged.

Elizabeth turned her eyes to Captain Larkin and seemed to steel herself to speak of the topic. "I did not like him, and it seemed that speaking with him made my father angry or sad, but I was not afraid of him until the last time he came to visit. He was so angry, pacing the floor and saying terrible things in his soft voice. Father was very ill by then, and could barely rise from his chair, but the man said that his condition would hardly excuse him for failing to fulfill their agreement. He snatched a doll from the shelf. It was an old one," she said as if to excuse herself. "I don't play with it any longer. I haven't for a long while."

"Of course not," Marianne soothed although she had seen the girl clutching the doll in her sleep. "Just tell us what happened."

She took another settling breath. "He told Father to have a care lest he grow so displeased that his anger be forced to find vent on Father's associates. 'You would do well to remember that her safety is only ensured if I am satisfied, for a turncoat cannot very well cry for assistance from the country he has betrayed, can he?' he said, and then—" Elizabeth broke off into barely suppressed sobs.

Captain Larkin stood and began to pace.

"Take your time," said Doctor Larkin reassuringly as once more. "We have all the time in the world for you to collect yourself a little and take a few nice deep breaths."

Marianne was not entirely convinced of that, for as Elizabeth pressed a tearful face into her shoulder, she caught sight of Captain Larkin' expression. The word 'turncoat' might as well have been a dagger to his heart, she realized, and he looked as though he might be ill. Between Elizabeth's sobs and his mute agony, Marianne felt sympathetic tears rising to her own eyes, but she dashed them away quickly when Elizabeth took a deep, if quaking breath, and composed herself to finish recounting the incident.

"Father wasn't a turncoat," she said hiccupping. "He wasn't."

"Of course not," Marianne soothed stroking the girl's hair.

Captain Larkin, she noticed seemed to be holding himself like a taut bow. "Please continue, Elizabeth," he said in a firm tone, which was not harsh, but brooked no quarter.

Marianne was proud of the way Elizabeth gathered herself and continued.

"Perhaps it does not sound very frightening," Elizabeth said, "but once he said that, the man twisted the head off of my doll and threw her body against the wall. He placed her glass head, oh so carefully on the table Then he placed his hand on my own neck, very gently, he did not actually hurt me at all, but I could scarcely draw a breath. I was so frightened. His hand was so large. I can still feel the ghost of his fingers against my throat, his thumb rubbing up and down until he pushed it under my chin and forced me to look at him. His eyes were so terribly cold, and his fingers so strong. I knew he wanted to kill me right there and then. His fingers tightened, and I wanted to scream, but I couldn't even move. It seemed he had already choked the breath from me although he had done nothing wrong.

"Father stood, so suddenly he knocked over the chair, but he was weak and had to hold on to the table. Father told the man to unhand me, but he only laughed. Then he told Father that a fortnight was all the additional time he would give him. He marched towards and door, but paused. 'You, my dear, he said, I will visit again, if your father reneges. A fortnight,' he repeated.

"The whole affair upset Father so much that it brought on one of his terrible spells, coughing so terribly and for so long that the innkeeper sent for the doctor."

Elizabeth paused closing her eyes against the tears that threatened. When she spoke again, her voice was soft, filled with grief. "Father died not three days later, and I knew, I couldn't stay at the inn. I knew I had to get away with all haste. I had to run before a fortnight was up."

PART IV

CHAPTER 23

The small group seemed to hold their breath with the tale. This young child had seen so much, endured so much in her short lifetime. Marianne's heart went out to her. Yes, her own mother had died, but she still had her father, and she had her safety. She forced back the emotions. She needed to think of this logically to protect the girl.

"Did you ever see the man after that visit?" asked Marianne, seeing that Captain Larkin was unable to speak. "When you were traveling, perhaps, or after you arrived here?"

"No. I have been terribly afraid that he would find me here, and perhaps hurt one of you if I could not give him whatever it was that he wanted from Father."

"You are safe here, Elizabeth," said Captain Larkin staunchly, recovering himself with a great effort. "Put your mind to rest on that front. I will see that no harm comes to you or to anyone else." He glanced toward Marianne and then back to his ward. "Do you know what it was, exactly, that the man did want from your father?"

"My only idea is that it must be some sort of papers. That was what Father had given him in the past, and he had given Father a packet of bank notes in return," answered the girl, unaware of just how damning those words were. The adults exchanged glances over her head. "But there was nothing like that left in Father's things, at least not that I found."

"I think you are an extraordinarily brave young lady," said Doctor Larkin briskly, providing a distraction from the vicious curse that sprang from his brother's lips. "That sounds to me like an utterly terrifying experience, heightened, I have no doubt, by the grief that followed so shortly afterwards. It would be a great deal more surprising to me if you had *not* been suffering from nightmares. But I suspect they will abate now that you have confided in us, and you no longer have to worry about it all alone. Did you ever mention any of this to Daphne, or to anyone else, for that matter?"

"No," Elizabeth whispered, flushing red. "I wanted to pretend that none of it ever happened. It was enough to manage that during my waking hours, for it all seemed impossible. I don't care what that man said, my father would never betray his country. It isn't true, and so I made myself think that the rest of it was untrue as well. It must be untrue," she said with conviction.

"Of course, my dear," murmured the doctor, shooting a concerned glance in the direction of his brother. "You see now, though, how such things have an unpleasant way of refusing to be ignored? One way or another they will force themselves into the light. Can you think of anything else that you have not mentioned here, anything else that might trouble your mind in slumber?"

But Elizabeth shook her head and remained firm on that point. She had nothing else to reveal, and Marianne was inclined to believe her, for the child's relief was palpable and undeniable.

"Dearest, why don't you run and fetch Ellen back for us?" she suggested. "And then you and Daphne might as well have some tea, for I rather suspect that you will not be leaving anytime soon."

"Andrew," began Doctor Larkin in a firm voice the instant that the little girl exited the room. His brother scowled at him and turned to stalk, stiff-shouldered and filled with tension, to the window.

Marianne could see his powerful-looking fists clenching into white-knuckled fists, and she found it took scarcely any effort at all to imagine him venting his feelings on whatever hapless furniture stood nearby. After a quick assessment of the furnishings she decided that nothing particularly irreplaceable or sentimental was within the captain's immediate vicinity and gave a slight shrug at the idea.

"There is no need to 'Andrew' me in that warning tone, Roger," said Captain Larkin after a tense moment. "I have a better rein on my temper than I once did, and I will certainly not disrespect Lady Marianne's hospitality by letting it loose here and now."

"Honestly, there is nothing in this room that we are particularly attached to, if you *need* to smash something," Marianne remarked, drawing a baffled half-laugh from the furious man. "I understand."

"I have already mentioned today that you are an exceedingly unusual creature, Lady Marianne, but the comment seems to bear repeating. I would doubtless be tempted to take you up on that offer if I believed for even an instant that Southampton was a turncoat, but the fact of the matter is that such a thing is utterly impossible."

"Playing the devil's advocate seems a rather risky proposition at the moment," said Doctor Larkin cautiously. "In spite of what seems to have been a particularly damning account of your friend. Perhaps instead, you will permit me to ask why you are so certain of his innocence?"

"Because I knew his character every bit as well as I know yours, brother. Disloyalty in any form was simply antithetical to Henry's very nature. I will not deny that the evidence otherwise does look quite compelling, but it makes no difference to me, for I *know*. If someone recited a great mountain of arguments that seemed to prove that the sun rose in the West, you would still not entertain the idea, would you? It is the same in this case and no one need waste their breath telling me otherwise."

"I will not, then. But what other explanation can be given to interpret this particular mountain of arguments?" asked the doctor gently.

"A very simple explanation, I should think," Marianne said, unable to keep silent in the presence of such a conversation. Both brothers turned to her with nearly identical expressions of surprise.

"You believe me, then, Lady Marianne?" demanded Captain Larkin, crossing the room to her, and speaking with great intensity. "I confess that I had not looked for that, considering the logical and factual bent of your mind."

"If you are saying that it is a fact that your friend could never betray his country, then of course I am willing to examine the matter from just that perspective," she retorted, a little nettled at the implication that she was ruled by cold logic alone. "It would be exceedingly narrow-minded to bind oneself to a conclusion that disregards such an informed testimony of character. Perhaps you *are* mistaken, and Lieutenant Southampton has pulled the wool over your eyes over the course of many years, in and out of life and death situations requiring absolute trust in one's comrades, but that seems highly unlikely to me. You trusted the man with your life. He trusted you with his daughter."

"What is this simple explanation that you propose, then?" wondered the doctor curiously.

"Why, that for the exact reasons that Lieutenant Southampton seems on the surface to be an ideal candidate for defecting from his country—his reduced financial circumstances, a young child to provide for and protect, a sudden and fatal illness—he was perfectly placed to act as a sort of decoy turncoat."

"There may be something to that idea," Doctor Larkin agreed thoughtfully. "He certainly seemed to have that Fumèe fellow convinced, at the very least. But it would surely be a difficult undertaking to prove that particular theory. Not that there seems to be a very pressing need to prove it, since the lieutenant has not been officially accused of anything or denounced by our country."

"I dislike the idea that any truth is improvable," Marianne said with a casual shrug that belied just how much she disliked that idea.

"I could never rest with such a thing hanging over Henry's reputation," added Captain Larkin, not taking his eyes from Marianne's face for even an instant. "My honor will not allow it, and besides that, there is Elizabeth's future to consider. If such an accusation is ever made, it will be a blight on her name and prospects. But I will admit that finding proof is not the *most* urgent matter just now. Regardless of Henry's guilt or innocence, Fumèe believes my friend was in possession of some valuable information, and I can assure you both that the spy will never relent until he has recovered it."

"Do you mean to say that you believe he will come here in search of whatever it is your friend may or may not have possessed?" the doctor's sharp tone, in contrast with his usually unflappable manner, sent a chill of dismay up Marianne's spine. She could see from Captain

Larkin' grim expression that the unpleasant idea seemed likely to him, which was far from comforting.

"It is almost certain that he will do just that. Indeed, I cannot imagine what has detained him this long, for it could not have been a terribly difficult matter to get Elizabeth's intended destination from the inn keeper. But mark my words, he will inevitably make his appearance, or barring that, since Elizabeth has actually seen his face, he will send another agent in his stead. Then she will be in very real danger from some unknown source."

It was on the tip of Marianne's tongue to protest that surely not even a hardened spy and villain such as la Fumèe would go so far as to harm a child, but she realized the folly of that notion and kept silent. From everything she had heard it seemed that evil would be a minor consideration to a man of that character.

At that moment, Ellen returned, looking a little flustered.

"Well, you all look unpromisingly grim," she remarked, going immediately to her fiancée's side. "I halfway do not even want to know what you have discovered, although of course I should die of curiosity if no one told me. But first, Marianne, there is a terribly handsome, scholarly looking creature searching for you."

"Oh. It is Sir Henry. You have not actually met him yet, Ellen. The poor man, I have forgotten about him entirely this morning," Marianne exclaimed in consternation. "He *is* a scholar, from Oxford, here to examine one of those scrolls that Arabella and Christopher brought me back from Greece."

"He is quite charming, and wandering about looking rather like a lost puppy," laughed Ellen, although she attempted to quell her amusement quickly once she caught sight of Captain Larkin' expression.

"Lost puppy indeed," he muttered, looking thunderous. Suddenly his entire manner changed, and he caught Marianne's wrist in his hand before she could exit the room. "Stay, a moment."

The order was so filled with authority that Marianne did not even think of resisting, but simply stared at the captain in amazement.

"Andrew, really," began Doctor Larkin, but his brother cut off the objection with a piercing look.

"Lady Marianne, had you ever actually met Sir Henry before this visit?" he demanded urgently.

"Why, no, we have only corresponded before now. Actually, it is rather amusing in hindsight, although I did not find it so at the time, but Sir Henry was under the mistaken assumption I was a man until he arrived."

"I am certain that it was highly amusing, and certainly put you off of your guard," retorted Captain Larkin.

"Should I have been *on* my guard?" Marianne felt utterly baffled by the statement, and by the barely constrained violence that she could almost palpably feel coursing from the man who still held her by the wrist.

"Think of the timing, Lady Marianne. This gentleman you have never met shows up conveniently just now, when Elizabeth is here, and disarms you so that you do not take the time to verify his identity or credentials?"

"You think he is working for la Fumèe? But—"

"I knew there was a good reason that I took such an instinctive dislike to the man. And now he is wandering the house freely, with all but unlimited access to Elizabeth. Where is she, Ellen?"

"I left her and Daphne with plans to tease the cook for some sweets," Ellen answered, rather reluctantly.

Captain Larkin released Marianne's wrist and rushed from the room, his expression boding ill indeed for Sir Henry.

Marianne stared after him wide eyed.

CHAPTER 24

"Ah, and there we have it," Doctor Larkin said with a resigned sigh. "Your furnishings have escaped being the object of Andrew's wrath, but I daresay that Sir Henry will not be so fortunate, should Andrew locate him before his anger cools down."

"But the entire idea is preposterous," Marianne said, barely keeping herself from wringing her hands in helpless distress. "Of course, Sir Henry is who he claims to be. You can hardly portray yourself fraudulently as a scholar of antiquities, not while examining and discussing and translating for such an extended period of time."

"An excellent point – although I would imagine that it could also be reasoned that Sir Henry Downing is precisely who he claims to be *and* is employed by the spy," suggested the doctor. "But perhaps we had better leave off this discussion until after we have located Sir Henry and intervened?"

A crash and a shout ringing out in the distance underscored Doctor Larkin's words, and Marianne could only agree with him wordlessly as they hastened out of the room in search for the two gentlemen.

"There you are, Marianne, you are missing all the fun." cried Daphne as soon as she caught sight of her sister. "Captain Larkin seems to be determined to frighten Sir Henry out of his wits. It is terribly entertaining, but Elizabeth and I thought we had better fetch someone to stop him before he does any real lasting damage."

The unrepentant regret in Daphne's tone at missing an exciting event such as a brawl in their very own home, would have made Marianne laugh at any other time, but at that moment she could only rush down the passageway that Daphne indicated. She arrived at the threshold of the kitchen just in time to see Doctor Larkin helping Sir Henry up from the floor, where he lay in a jumble of broken crockery. The kitchen staff were all looking on with avid excitement, and Captain Larkin seemed not a whit calmer as he watched his foe wipe blood from his battered lip with an air of supreme confusion.

"Oh, really, you *struck* him?" Marianne exclaimed in exasperation. "That cannot possibly have been necessary, Captain Larkin."

"This man is in all likelihood a spy in the employ of a foreign enemy, here with ill intent towards my ward, and moreover he was running from me. Would you rather I had allowed him to escape?"

"I think I can hardly be blamed for running when someone comes racing at me, hand on hilt, looking bent on destruction," Sir Henry retorted, as tartly as possible through the swelling of his lip.

"My lady," the cook said, in a tone that warned Marianne of far greater destruction if the kitchen were allowed to be disrupted any further.

"I do apologize," she said quickly. "Come, let us take this discussion elsewhere, gentlemen, if you will all be so courteous?"

The three men followed her rather sheepishly, as she led the way out of the kitchen, thinking that there must be something terribly wrong with her priorities because at the moment she felt more worried that the cook would leave than anything else. She had lost entirely too much staff already. She would not let this abide.

"Well, I would say there is no harm done, but I have been on the receiving end of that blow myself a time or two growing up," said Doctor Larkin cheerfully enough as he assisted the scholar to a seat. "It really is like nothing so much as being charged by a mad bull, I believe."

"If I have given offence in any way I most sincerely apologize, it was entirely inadvertent, I can assure you all," replied Sir Henry, looking directly at Marianne he spoke.

"I do not believe *you* have anything to apologize for, Sir Henry," she replied rather pointedly. "It is my belief that this is all merely a misunderstanding—compounded by rash action. Captain Larkin, if you had but stayed a moment, I would have explained to you that it is quite impossible that Sir Henry is an imposter. He is, indeed, a very knowledgeable and dedicated scholar. I have seen ample evidence of that with my own eyes. I suppose I must apologize for not insisting that you stay and listen to me, but really, I had no notion that your method of investigation would be to strike first."

"As I said before, he ran from me. It seems only logical to presume it was an indication of his guilt," the captain said, still obviously struggling to control his temper. "If you say that he is truly a scholar then I shall of course believe you. However, that alone does not rule out his guilt or involvement in this matter. Any recent newcomer to the village *must* be considered as suspect, particularly one who makes a point of seeking out *this* home and *this* family."

"I beg your pardon, but did you say something about a spy earlier?" interjected Sir Henry, wide eyed. "You surely are not saying that you think I am working against our kingdom?"

"I have ample evidence that there is, in fact, motivation for a spy to infiltrate this household. The abrupt timing of your visit certainly merits further scrutiny," returned the captain rather stiffly, as if attempting to regain some semblance of dignity.

"And my conveniently suspicious timing gives you a much-desired excuse to impugn my character, I see, it is all perfectly clear now," shot back Sir Henry hotly. He could never hope to best Captain Larkin in a physical contest, but he looked quite ready to make an attempt, Marianne thought with some alarm.

"Do not be ridiculous. Why ever should I desire an excuse to impugn your character?"

"It is hardly ridiculous to observe that you desire no rivals for Lady Marianne's affection and attention," Sir Henry answered, flushing with embarrassment. "That is quite understandable in and of itself, but your methods, sir, are hardly worthy of your rank. Might I suppose you have also assaulted Mr. Baxley in a similar manner? Or perhaps you do not consider him so much of a threat."

"That is hardly—" Captain Larkin began furiously, shaking off his brother's restraining arm, but Marianne interposed herself between the two angry gentlemen. If indeed, she reflected wryly, they could be termed as such at that particular moment.

"Sir Henry, you are of course right to wish to defend your honor against an accusation of treason, but I fear you have misread the dynamic of this situation. Captain Larkin has never expressed any interest in such a thing, and is most certainly *not* motivated by any sense of rivalry, I can assure you."

"Indeed," said the scholar, quite skeptically, after a painfully long moment. "I shall, of course, take your opinion as fact, Lady Marianne. But I am quite at a loss as to how I may prove my innocence in the face of these unfounded charges."

"That will hardly be necessary," Doctor Larkin interposed in his calm and soothing way, aiming a quelling look at Captain Larkin even as he spoke to Sir Henry. "You must accept our apologies for this unfortunate interlude, Sir Henry, and I pray you will not harbor *too* much resentment at my brother's treatment. He is quite distressed at the possibility that his ward may be in danger."

"Such vigilance is, I suppose, rather admirable," conceded Sir Henry, although he continued to return Captain Larkin' glare with equal ferocity.

"One hopes," agreed the doctor amiably. "Perhaps I might convince you to accept a poultice to reduce the bruising and swelling on your face? It will only take me a few moments to prepare."

Sir Henry looked as though he wanted to deny that he was in any pain from the blow, but conceded with a quick nod after a brief internal struggle between comfort and pride. The doctor led him from the room, sparing a bemused backward glance at his brother.

"Lady Marianne—" Captain Larkin began, his voice intense, but Marianne cut him off mercilessly. She was far too overwhelmed and bewildered to hear anything that he, or indeed, *anyone*, had to say at that moment.

"Captain Larkin, if you still have the letter from Lieutenant Southampton that Elizabeth brought with her, perhaps you might read over it again considering this new information. Perhaps there is some sort of clue hidden there that you did not notice at first. And I think you had better take her back with you after all, so that you may better keep watch over her," she said firmly, not quite able summon up the courage to meet his eyes.

"Very well," he responded, in a tone that clearly showed that he wished to argue the point further. "My sincerest apologies for causing such trouble in your home."

Marianne could only nod her acknowledgement, suddenly afraid that her voice would betray the rush of tears that she could feel closing her throat. She was grateful that he did not press the issue, and that Ellen led him out of the room, offering to collect Elizabeth, before her composure failed altogether.

CHAPTER 25

"I have had a most fascinating visit from Ellen," Arabella announced without preamble when she let herself into Marianne's chamber a few hours later.

Marianne lifted her eyes to her sister, but found that she could not, despite having devoted the time to gathering and ordering her thoughts, think of anything to say.

"Naturally I came here at once, and before I could find you, I was waylaid by the housekeeper, who *also* had a fascinating tale to relate to me. The staff has had a marvelously exciting day, from what I understand," Arabella continued, undaunted by Marianne's silence.

"Oh no, I forgot to speak to the cook," Marianne groaned. "Of course, she will be hideously upset at the incident in the kitchen, and I ought to have gone to soothe her feelings immediately. But really, it is too much to expect that I should think of such a thing while

I'm in the middle of nightmares, possible treason, murderous spies, and guests assaulting one another and who knows what else."

"Well, you've left out declarations of affection, for one thing," laughed Arabella. "From Ellen's recounting of the incident, it would seem that Sir Henry all but proclaimed his eternal love for you on bended knee, and the captain darkened his daylights. But do not worry about the staff, dearest, for I have already spoken with them all. The cook *was* rather irate, and you may perhaps expect a rather simpler dinner than usual this evening. She mentioned something about a soup scorching, a cake falling flat, and various other culinary catastrophes directly resulting from having a brawl take place in her kitchen. But I was able to mollify her. And none of the new maids were horrified enough to take their leave. Indeed, I think they are really rather pleased at the prospect of working someplace where handsome young men may burst into the kitchen in such a spectacular manner at odd times." Arabella grinned at her with undisguised merriment.

"There is always a silver lining, I suppose. But I daresay that Ellen's account was nearly as excitable as that of the maids, for Sir Henry really did no such thing. He seemed to think – falsely, of course – that Captain Larkin was eager to accuse him out of misplaced jealousy. It is a logical enough conclusion, even though Captain Larkin has never had such an idea in his life."

"I am not altogether convinced that he hasn't, but I will leave that alone for the time being. Do you *really* believe that Sir Henry did not arrive at that conclusion via some other route than pure logic?" asked Arabella, giving Marianne a piercing gaze.

"I...that is, I don't know," Marianne faltered, unable to conceal her own confusion from her sister. "It perhaps *did* seem, at the time, that his words and manner implied that he had some sort of... interest in me. It was a very overwrought moment, though, and I cannot be certain that I interpreted everything accurately, you know."

"Of course, and I daresay that the closest interpretation lies somewhere between your own tendency to assume that gentlemen are not interested in you, and Ellen's rather more romantic and fanciful view of the world. But really, Marianne, you cannot deny that Sir Henry *has* seemed markedly impressed by your many charms ever since he arrived here."

"I don't know, perhaps you are right, but there is not enough evidence to say conclusively," Marianne hedged.

"Very well if you are determined to be stubborn and pedantic on that point," said Arabella with some asperity. "But take it as a hypothetical case then, and tell me what you imagine your feelings might be *if* Sir Henry were to make a declaration?"

"I suppose...hypothetically, of course, that I would be inclined to give such a declaration some serious thought. Sir Henry seems as if he might be rather ideally suited to me in some ways."

"Because he is handsome, intelligent, and courteous, and moreover has devoted his life to study, and values your intellect highly without consideration of your gender?" suggested Arabella with a smile.

"Yes, principally," Marianne agreed, smiling in return. "I should not have thought it possible that such a man existed. Do you really think he might feel favorably towards me?"

"I think it is blindingly obvious that he finds you to be both fascinating and ideally suited to *him*. But what are *your* feelings towards the gentleman?"

"I hardly know—" began Marianne, blushing, but she was cut short by Daphne, who burst into the room with a scowl and an aggrieved air.

"Marianne, one of your admirers has bid me to fetch you so that he may discuss his intentions," she stated, throwing herself petulantly into a chair.

"Who do you mean?" Marianne asked.

"Do not answer that question just yet, Daphne," interposed Arabella swiftly, her voice firm enough to check whatever Daphne had been about to say. "Before she does, Marianne, you must admit that this is the perfect opportunity to discern something important for yourself. Who did you *hope* she meant, the moment she spoke? That answer ought to tell you all that you need to know about your own feelings."

"Oh, I see," murmured Marianne, struck by the idea.

"Well?" Daphne demanded, immediately distracted from her pique.

Marianne considered, but forcibly halted her thoughts before the mental image could fully form. *That* was not information she actually wanted to deal with at the moment.

"Well, nothing," she said with a scowl, refusing to acknowledge the real answer. "The experiment did not work, so never mind about it. Who *is* here?"

Arabella seemed to be on the point of arguing further, but Daphne answered Marianne's question before she could press the issue.

"It is the ever-so-delightful Mr. Baxley, of course. He would have been here hours ago only something kept him. I don't know what. He recited a very long and dull narrative, and I was doing my very best not to attend to it."

"Never mind," said Marianne. "But why do you say that he is here to discuss his intentions?"

"Because he said so, in those exact words," snorted Daphne. "I unfortunately *was* listening to that bit, because he caught my attention when he started talking about his great delight at the idea of soon being my brother. My *brother*. Why, I should never consider calling him that even if you did lose your mind and agree to marry the ridiculous creature."

"Did you say that?" Arabella wanted to know, although she looked more amused than horrified at the thought of Daphne unleashing her wrath on the man.

"I was scarcely given the opportunity to say anything. I *began* to say I was very surprised to hear him speak in such a way, for I had not heard a word of those tidings. But the odious man cut me off with the most condescending little speech about how children are not privy to the serious discussions of their adult family members, that it had already been settled. The beastly man said I was not to worry or alarm myself but to just run and fetch my sister so the last few little details may be decided. And then he *patted my head*."

"And yet he lives? Does this mean that there is now a gentleman currently bleeding all over the drawing room?"

"I thought I might get in trouble if I removed his hand, from both my head *and* his arm, as I was first inclined to," Daphne said with a feline smile. "So, I decided to content myself with watching Marianne deflate his preposterous assumptions. Perhaps I may twist the knife a bit when he is on his way out."

"I fear it may take an actual knife to deflate Baxley's assumptions," said Marianne in great exasperation. "I hardly have the time or inclination to bother with this after everything else that has happened today, but I suppose I must or else I will turn around and find myself actually married to him."

"How is it possible for anyone to be so outrageously self-assured?" wondered Arabella. "Neither you nor Father has given him the slightest encouragement, yet he feels that the match has already been made. I'm afraid you shall have to count me in your audience, as well as

Daphne – for the sake of having a witness as much as for the sake of my own entertainment. Actually, perhaps we had better just have Father deal with him."

"I would love to, but of course Father is not yet back from his trip to London, and he did not give me any indication as to his return," Marianne sighed. "I will have to do it myself. I don't mind an audience, for I hardly think that the odious man's delicate feelings deserve any consideration at this point. You must promise to stop him if he shows signs of reciting the wedding vows. I wouldn't put it past him, honestly."

CHAPTER 26

"Ah, behold the most radiant of all creatures," Mr. Baxley exclaimed when Marianne entered the drawing room. How he could call her such when she knew her expression to be particularly grim, not to mention the ravages that a distressing morning and a bout of weeping must have caused to her face, belied all reason. She could feel her hair hanging down her back, released from its pins. The man's beatific smile fairly beamed at her like the sun as he crossed the room to press her hands in his.

"Good afternoon, sir, I hope you are well?" Marianne said in the most formal and cold tone possible, pulling her hands swiftly from his grasp.

"Well, is not a word to describe my state of being, now that I am in the presence of my beloved," he gushed effusively. "But perhaps we might speak in private?"

"That would hardly be proper, I am afraid, but you may rest assured my sisters are not prone to gossip, and there is nothing we may say that I would wish to conceal from them."

"You are marvelously correct, my dear, marvelously. Of course, we must observe all standards of propriety even now. I shall bow to your whim, of course. But you know, once we are wed, I should hope that you will accept that my knowledge of such matters is quite extensive, and you can trust my judgement."

"Once we are wed?" Marianne asked stiffly, surprised in spite of herself at his presumption.

"Yes, of course, my dear. That is just the sort of thing I wished to discuss today, the details of our union. I am of the belief that it is wise to examine and communicate such expectations that a husband and wife may have of one another in advance, to achieve a better understanding of one another."

"That is an admirable goal, I am sure, Mr. Baxley. But a rather lofty one, for we clearly do not understand one another whatsoever at present."

"Why, I cannot imagine why you might think such a thing," he protested genially. "I am certain that no matter how vast the differences between the masculine and feminine minds may be, a clever lady such as yourself will not find the task *too* mystifying. Do not allow yourself to become daunted by the task, my dear."

"I confess I am entirely mystified," Marianne managed to say, ignoring Daphne's stifled giggling behind her.

"As for being daunted, I imagine the task would seem rather overwhelming, if indeed it were one to which I was inclined to apply myself. Thankfully it is not, for I cannot begin to imagine what you are thinking of, sir, in assuming that there is any understanding between you and me."

"Whatever can you mean by that, I wonder?" Mr. Baxley looked genuinely surprised by her firm tone.

"Simply that your presumption that there might ever be a union between us is both unwarranted and unwelcome. I am sorry to have to speak so plainly, but I cannot allow your confusion to continue any longer," she said calmly, watching the man's color rise and fade for a moment.

"Now, now, my dear, do not become overwrought," he said, his voice so filled with condescension that Marianne could actually feel her palms tingle with the urge to strike him. "It is natural for you to become emotional and illogical at such an exciting time as this, but you must do your best to control such hysterical tendencies, you know."

"It is very odd that you would accuse me of being overwrought or emotional. I am not raising my voice or crying or displaying any other signs that might indicate such a state," Marianne observed, tilting her head a little to the side as she studied the gentleman. "I suppose I might attribute your mistaken perception to the fact that I am a woman, and therefore in your eyes weak-minded and given to hysteria, and moreover that I am saying something that you do not wish to hear. Regardless of the explanation, however, you really must attend to what I am saying for you are embarrassing us both."

"Indeed, you are quite mistaken, Lady Marianne. I have the highest respect for womankind, I can assure you of that. I am generously ascribing your sudden change of heart to those feminine tendencies I mentioned, rather than assuming that you are guilty of being a fickle, flirtatious creature," he exclaimed, staring at Marianne as if he had never seen her before, which, she reflected, was entirely accurate.

"I have given you no indication that I returned your sudden, groundless interest. And I say groundless, quite deliberately," she added, seeing that he was about to interrupt her to argue that point. "For you do not know me beyond the briefest of acquaintances. You know I meet certain requirements that you have in mind for your ideal bride, but I can assure you that beyond those surface qualities I would be the least likely woman in the kingdom to please you. As for my being fickle or flirtatious, you will see if you are capable of genuine retrospect and reflection, that I have engaged in no interaction with you that could possibly be construed as such. I do not return your affection, nor would I if we were to spend years growing better acquainted. It is really quite simple, you see. I do not want to marry you."

"I have already spoken with your father, you know, and *he*—"

"And he gave you no more encouragement than I have," Marianne interposed. "You have no one to blame for your misunderstanding other than yourself, I am afraid.

Perhaps you will reflect on this distressing episode and apply it in your future pursuits, but I rather doubt you will do anything so sensible as that. Therefore, we really have nothing further to say to one another."

"My dear, you are far too hasty and impulsive. Your father has indulged you, I have no doubt, and allowed you to develop some rather unfortunate and headstrong habits. Your wits may be a bit sharper than those of your peers, but I fear you have muddled your thoughts with too much study. I do not hold it against you, of course. Indeed, I have every intention of indulging your little studies as well, knowing that their fascination will soon pale in comparison to the delights of being a wife and mother."

"Sir, I cannot understand why you persist in this insulting conversation, for I am very plainly rejecting your advances," said Marianne, amazed at the man.

"There now, you *are* becoming overwrought, just as I said. Perhaps it would be best if I speak to Lord Sedgewick about the details, it was a mistake to burden your delicate mind with them, I see," he said soothingly.

Out of the corner of her eye, Marianne could see Daphne make a sudden movement, presumably to launch herself at the man. Before she could make up her mind to intervene, however, Captain Larkin strode into the room.

CHAPTER 27

"Lady Marianne, I hope you will forgive my interruption, but I have made absolutely no progress whatsoever with this encryption and I must beg for your assistance," the captain declared unexpectedly, his tone mild but his steely gaze fixed pointedly on Baxley's face. "I am hopeless at such things as riddles and puzzles, but I at least have the wits to know when a problem is beyond my capability and defer it to a superior resource. Only a very great fool indeed could fail to recognize that you possess a level of brilliance and acuity unparalleled by any person hereabouts."

"I...ah, yes, of course," stammered Marianne, entirely thrown off course by both his sudden appearance and his speech.

"I beg your pardon, Captain Larkin, but I do not believe I care for the insinuation," declared Mr. Baxley, drawing himself up more pompously than ever, if such a thing were even possible.

"My mistake, sir, for my intention was not to insinuate anything," the captain replied. "For I did not trust that a person as thoroughly oblivious as yourself might be capable of grasping an insinuation. I *meant* to state outright that you are a great fool."

"Really, now."

"Lady Marianne, I can only imagine that my presence here is distasteful to you," he continued, utterly ignoring the blustering Mr. Baxley. "And rightfully so, a fact which I regret far more than I can say. I had not intended to distress you with my company. I was going to leave the encrypted letter with a note asking for your assistance, but then I could not help but overhearing this unpleasant conversation. I have no doubt that you are more than capable of ridding yourself of an unwanted and persistent suitor without my aid, so I fear I have been overzealous once more and I apologize."

Marianne could have sworn that she felt her heart trip at the captain's words, and she felt a little dizzy as she met his eyes. Fortunately, the presence of the odious Mr. Baxley made it impossible for her to become *too* lost in foolish emotions, as his sputtering protests were far too adamant to ignore.

"I do not believe that this gentleman's misplaced confidence, powerful as it is, has the ability to hypnotize me into agreeing to something against my wishes," she murmured. "But I must admit that your assistance is both timely and welcome."

"Come now, my dear, you do not know what you are saying. You are confused and distraught—"

"I will not allow you to continue to speak so insultingly to Lady Marianne, in her own home, no less," snapped Captain Larkin in an entirely different tone than the one which he had just used to address Marianne. Even directed at someone other than herself, she felt her spine stiffen automatically in alarm, and she could see the color drain entirely out of Baxley's already doughy white face.

"Insultingly?" he stammered, fairly cringing away from the furious military man. "You are quite mistaken, I assure you—"

"I assure *you* that I am in no way mistaken. You are a greater fool than I thought, which defies all reason, but there it is. If you cannot see that your repeated condescending denigration of Lady Marianne's intellect is nothing short of the rankest insult. She, more than anyone of my acquaintance, knows perfectly well what she is saying at all times. And I have *no doubt* that she has greater control of her emotions than anyone in this room. It is utter nonsense to claim otherwise, simply because the fact does not align with your own ridiculous ideas."

"Now, surely you cannot mean to say that even the brightest of women can even begin to equal a man in matters of intellect," protested Baxley. "Why, the very idea is preposterous."

"I am not overburdened with education, myself, but I can see nothing preposterous in the idea. I am exceedingly well-versed in military strategies, however, and therefore am able to see that there is no point whatsoever in continuing this interview further. Lady Marianne, do you wish to marry Baxley?"

"No, thank you," Marianne managed to answer, torn between amazement and a strong desire to laugh.

"There you have it, sir. I have unfortunately already committed one act of violence in this home today and have no wish to repeat my uncivilized behavior, but if you persist in ignoring the lady's wishes I will have no choice. Good day, Mr. Baxley," added the captain, with such a force of command ringing in his voice that the man involuntarily started towards the door.

"Oh, dear, I suppose this means that you will not be my brother after all," exclaimed Daphne in a mockingly sweet voice. The man glared at her furiously for an instant and then marched out of the room, slamming the door ungraciously behind himself.

"Thank you," Marianne repeated, turning her attention back to Captain Larkin after staring at the door in amazement for a moment. "He really would not hear a word that I was saying. It was exceedingly frustrating and confusing."

"I am pleased to have been able to render some small assistance, although I admit I was tempted to hold back a little longer just to see Miss Daphne launch her own attack. But perhaps preventing one act of violence will partially atone for committing another earlier," he replied soberly.

"You don't...you don't think Baxley *could* be working with la Fumèe? It would certainly be a diabolically clever cover."

"As much as I would love an excuse to interrogate the pompous creature, I am afraid he is almost entirely above suspicion in that area, for I checked his credentials after I left here this morning," confessed the captain ruefully. "Besides, he would hardly press his suit so foolishly if he were attempting to maintain a duplicitous presence."

"That is too bad, for it would have been a most satisfying outcome," laughed Arabella, breaking her unhelpful silence.

"Yes, indeed. Well, I will not stay any longer. I would not have come at all, but I have no hope of solving this encryption. I bid you all farewell, ladies," Captain Larkin said, rather uncomfortably, before handing the document to Marianne, clicking his heels and taking his leave.

Marianne had to check the impulse to stop him, to say something, anything, for it would have been in vain. Instead, she turned to her older sister with a scowl.

"Why ever are you angry at *me*?" asked Arabella, looking decidedly unrepentant.

"I did not realize that you meant to be a witness in such a literal sense of the word," said Marianne. "That interview might have gone on half the night if Captain Larkin had not made an appearance."

"I was going to come to your aid, truly I was, but then I happened to see the good captain coming along the passageway and I thought it would be eminently more interesting to see how he would intervene. And I was certainly right about that," Arabella replied with an arch look.

"He was quite marvelous, wasn't he?" agreed Daphne, and Marianne found herself sighing a little in agreement.

"Well, he was certainly more helpful than either of you," she snapped, once she realized that the sigh had been rather audible. "And to repay his assistance I had better get started on deciphering this letter before anything else ridiculous occurs."

She swept from the room and was nearly to the threshold of the library before realizing that even that most sacred of sanctuaries was now occupied, and she had no desire to speak with poor Sir Henry at the moment. Really, she reflected as she returned drearily to her own chamber, it was a pity that she did not have la Fumèe in her grasp at that precise moment, for nothing would have suited her mood better than a pitched battle with an uncomplicated foe.

CHAPTER 28

Marianne could not claim to feeling particularly cheerful or well-rested the next morning, but she was at least more composed than she had anticipated after yet another restless night. She could not even blame her sleeplessness on Elizabeth, although she had devoted a fair amount of her restless thoughts to worrying over the child.

It did surprise her when Sir Henry, looking pale and sadly bruised despite Doctor Larkin' ministrations, requested a conversation with her after breakfast.

"I really am terribly sorry for the incident yesterday," she began meekly. "It was a horrible misunderstanding, and I am mortified that such a thing occurred in my home-"

"Lady Marianne, I beg of you not to think of it," interrupted the scholar earnestly. "It was certainly none of your doing, and I cannot even fault your overly enthusiastic Captain Larkin, really, for he was only acting according to his nature."

"He is not *my* Captain Larkin," Marianne corrected automatically, and was surprised to see Sir Henry expression brighten considerably at her statement.

"In that case I have even less cause to bear the captain any ill-will. If he has no claim on your affections, then I can forgive him with the sincerest of generosity. I confess, too, that the altercation yesterday caused me to realize the strength of my own feelings."

Here Sir Henry paused, as if to give Marianne an opening to speak, but she could not think of any response to his statement. She realized, indeed, that he was on the point of making a declaration far more welcome than the one she had received the previous day, and was struck anew by the strangeness of receiving two proposals in as many days. When she remained silent, Sir Henry cleared his throat with an appealing look of uncertainty and continued.

"I know that our acquaintance has been very brief, and perhaps it is unforgivably presumptuous of me to say that you are the most admirable lady that I have ever met. I wish to make my intentions perfectly clear in the hopes that you might consider me, consider my suit, that is."

"Your suit," Marianne repeated, feeling that things had moved on apace and she was not ready for this eventuality.

Sir Henry nodded. "You are an intelligent woman. It cannot have escaped your notice, that I think highly of you."

She nodded. She did see that, although she was not at all sure what she wanted from this present encounter.

"For these last few days," he continued, "I have been able to think of little else than what our future together might be. Indeed, I have been dragging my feet with the authentication process simply for the sake of having an excuse to spend more time in your presence."

"I thought you were merely being particularly thorough," Marianne said, latching onto the side note in a desperate attempt to give herself more time to think. Sir Henry gave her a brilliant smile in response.

"I am always thorough, but in this particular case it was not really necessary. The scroll *is* authentic, I would gladly stake my reputation on it. Think, Lady Marianne, of the life and work we might build together. If the prospect appeals to you even in the slightest then you might give me some word of hope, for I do not mind waiting any length of time for you, such is the depth of my admiration," he said, taking her hand and gazing into her eyes with an expression of pure adoration. I have always felt I was married to my work. I never thought I would marry. No woman ever garnered my attention, until you, Lady Marianne. Together we could do great things. I think you see that."

Marianne *could* picture the life they might build together. The impossibly barred doors of academia would open to her as his companion, and she would have access to a wealth of information, lively discourse, and brilliant minds. He would respect her abilities, would appreciate her ideas and opinions in a way that few others might. No one could dream up a more ideal husband than the kind, patient, charming, and handsome Sir Henry Downing. It was a giddy, tempting prospect, and for a moment she saw the entirety of it flash before her eyes, comfortable, satisfying, and fulfilling. And yet, as she looked at their clasped hands, she realized that there was no flutter of anticipation in her heart. There was no molten heat flowing through her veins, and for most, the security of a marriage with Sir Henry would be more than enough, but for her, she did not think it would do. No, she realized, she was in love with Captain Larkin. But she wondered, was he in love with her? He had not stated his intentions. Would she be foolish to refuse Sir Henry when he was almost everything she wished in a husband? No, she thought. She could never do anything half-way, not even marriage.

"I like you, Sir Henry. I really do…"

"But you are in love with another," he said softly.

She nodded. "I am sorry, Sir Henry. Indeed, more sorry than I can possibly convey," she sighed, looking directly into his hopeful eyes, and feeling intensely wretched. "What you suggest sounds heavenly, and I wish more than anything that I might join you in such a tempting partnership, but I respect you far too much to do you such an injustice. I cannot love you, I am afraid, and it would be wrong of me to pretend otherwise or allow you to settle for less than you deserve."

"I have been too hasty, of course I do not expect you to feel as strongly as I do in such a short amount of time, there is no need for you to make a decision right away," he protested, but Marianne shook her head sadly.

"I fear that time will make no difference. Truly, I wish it were otherwise. I wish with all my heart that I might accept your offer. My rejection has nothing to do with you, for you are as good a man as I have ever met. I daresay the most perfect match I could ever hope to find. But matters of the heart do not fall in line with logic, do they?"

"I suppose they do not, which is perhaps the reason I have never before attempted to navigate them," Sir Henry replied, releasing her hands. "If you can give me no hope, I will of course respect your wishes, much as it pains me to do so. I will take my leave of you now, Lady Marianne, but do not hesitate to include my authentication when you publish your discovery. I will, of course, stand by our findings regardless of my personal disappointment, and Lady Marianne, your captain may be able to beat me to a pulp, but if he should ever hurt you…"

"Thank you," murmured Marianne softly, as he bowed and left the room. She was overwhelmed with emotion, yet strangely calm and detached. His proposal had given her a moment of perfect clarity, and she had not been able to silence or ignore it as she had done when

Arabella asked her who she hoped was requesting her presence.

"I've just seen Sir Henry in the passageway, and he bid me farewell, saying that he would be departing shortly," said Daphne, coming into the room and jolting Marianne out of her surreal moment of realization. "It is a terrible pity, for I quite like him."

"Yes, so do I," Marianne agreed, staring blindly out of the window. "It seems horribly unfair that I happen to love someone else so much more."

CHAPTER 29

As far as distractions went, deciphering the encrypted message in Lieutenant Southampton's final letter left much to be desired, Marianne decided. For one thing, the task was not terribly difficult and was over within the space of two hours. For another, completing it necessitated a visit to the very person she wished to distract herself from thinking of, but it could not be helped. Paying a call on the gentleman she had loved since she was a little girl – the gentleman who certainly would never return her affection – was unfortunately unavoidable, and Marianne had no intention of dragging out the unpleasant task any longer than was absolutely necessary.

Marching determinedly into Doctor Larkin's study, she was relatively pleased to find both the doctor and his brother sitting together.

"Good afternoon, Lady Marianne—" the two gentlemen began, rising to their feet at the sight of her, but Marianne cut the greeting short, impatient to deliver her message and get as far from Captain Larkin and his devilishly handsome face as possible. The painful twist that her heart gave at the sight of him was almost more than she could bear.

"Lieutenant Southampton was no traitor to the crown," she announced abruptly, handing the captain his letter and her note of translation.

"You don't mean to say you've broken the code already?" demanded Captain Larkin, taking her interruption in stride and staring at her excitedly. "Harry was well known for his ability to create puzzles and encryptions that were well-nigh impossible to decipher without the proper key."

"It was a very competent encryption," she agreed, keeping her voice flat and emotionless. "But yes, I have solved it. You will see in my translation that he was working with our government all along. His task was to appear destitute, presenting the façade of a man desperate for money and ripe for treason, so that *la Fumèe* or one of his ilk would seek him out. Having accomplished this, he then built his credibility by feeding the spy accurate documents and information – albeit things of lesser consequence – so that he could gradually seed the enemy with false information and eventually capture *la Fumèe*. The onslaught of his illness was so sudden that he had very little time to prepare for his death, but he gives the name of his superior in this scheme, who will be able to confirm his mission and clear his name if needed."

"That...that is incredible," Captain Larkin breathed, his air of relief so palpable that Marianne fancied she could actually *see* a weight lifting from his broad shoulders. "I feel ashamed for ever having considered that Harry could have betrayed his country, even for a moment."

"You did not really entertain the possibility," Doctor Larkin pointed out comfortingly. "You knew in your heart that he was a man of integrity."

"I did, but I felt it my duty to examine the matter as dispassionately as I was able. It is a greater relief than I can possibly say, to know that his integrity was as strong I believed it to be. I owe you a great debt of gratitude, Lady Marianne, one I cannot hope to repay."

"There is no need," Marianne answered shortly, mentally assigning the man's gratitude to perdition. "However, we are not quite finished with this matter, for I gathered from the lieutenant's message that *la Fumèe* remained unaware of his duplicity. The documents the spy is still seeking are both harmless and factually accurate things that the Crown does not mind leaking, but *la Fumèe* believes them to be valuable state secrets. The lieutenant states he concealed them within a broken doll which he planned to plant for the spy to find, ensuring that Elizabeth would not be pursued after his death."

"A clever plan," said the captain, frowning in consideration. "Elizabeth mentioned the spy breaking her doll as a threat when he visited, so finding documents in the doll would be something of a final insult. Thinking that Harry was taunting him with the idea that the papers he wanted had actually been within his grasp would most likely make *la Fumèe* believe he had won in the end."

"I suppose it might," Marianne said, her mind working furiously. "*If* the spy found the doll. But I rather wonder if he actually did. Doctor Larkin, we have assumed that Elizabeth's nightmares have been just that, a child's mind working through a frightening experience. But what if they, or at least some instances of them, were more concrete than that?"

"What are you suggesting? That her nightmares are actually happening?" demanded Captain Larkin before his brother could answer. His eyes widened in horror.

"Think about it for a moment," urged Marianne. "If Lieutenant Southampton was unable to plant the doll where *la Fumèe* could find it, the spy would rightfully assume that it was still in Elizabeth's possession. Might he not find some way of gaining access to her chamber at night, in order to search for it?"

She could see from the stricken expression on the captain's face that the proposed scenario was entirely possible. Without speaking another word, he strode from the room, calling for Elizabeth in an urgent tone.

"Has she had any more nightmares since returning here?" Marianne asked Doctor Larkin while they waited. He nodded grimly.

"Just one, last night, and she was quite hysterical with terror for some time. In fact, she was unable to go back to sleep until we gave her a bed in a different chamber."

Presently, Captain Larkin returned, with Elizabeth in tow. The little girl had a rather bewildered expression on her face, and she was clutching the decidedly battered doll that Marianne was used to seeing in her possession.

"Is something wrong?" asked the child timidly.

"Do not be alarmed, dearest," Marianne said soothingly. "This seems very odd, perhaps, but we have just realized that there are more questions about your frightening dreams and the man who visited your father. Is that the doll that the man broke that day, by any chance?"

"Yes," whispered Elizabeth, flushing guiltily. "Father tried to mend her for me after the man left, but he was coughing so much that he was unable to make much progress. He told me to never mind about her, that he would buy me a much better doll presently and put her in the bin. But I woke up in the middle of the night and saw him trying to mend her again. He put her back in the bin, so I supposed he was not pleased with the result. But he died the next morning, and I took her out and kept her. It was one of the very last things he did, you see, trying to set her right for me."

"Of course, you wanted to keep her, that is perfectly natural," Captain Larkin reassured the child. "I must ask you if we may examine your doll for a moment, but I promise to restore her to you shortly."

Elizabeth nodded, handing her precious possession trustingly to the captain, who looked comically awkward surveying the dainty offering.

"Lady Marianne?" he said after a moment, passing the doll to Marianne.

Parting the dress, Marianne revealed a row of rather clumsy stitches along the torso of the doll. Wordlessly, Doctor Larkin handed her a small pair of sharp scissors, which she used to undo the stitches. Elizabeth gave a little gasp of dismay, but Marianne smiled at her reassuringly.

"It will take not five minutes to set it right, I promise. But look here, I believe your father concealed something important within when he was mending her." Saying so, she gently worked a tightly rolled up letter from the depths of the doll and handed it to Captain Larkin, whose eyes were alight with sudden purpose.

"I had better return these to the officer Harry was reporting to. Harmless or not they should not be left lying around carelessly. In the meantime, however, I am given an idea as to how we may catch *la Fumèe* once and for all."

"Who is *la Fumèe*?" asked Elizabeth, her eyes wide.

"It is better that she be told, in my opinion," said Doctor Larkin once the adults had exchanged glances with one another. "Particularly if your theory is correct, Lady Marianne. I should not like to have it on my conscience that I encouraged a child to doubt her perceptions."

"Briefly, then," agreed his brother. "I do not wish you to become alarmed, Elizabeth, but the man you have been having such bad dreams of is a villainous man, and he wanted these papers. We think perhaps he has tried to search your chamber for them. Were there ever any of your nightmares that seemed like that?"

"Two or three times I dreamed he was standing in the room with me," Elizabeth said, her little face going white. "But I thought I was really still asleep and dreaming, for he vanished so quickly each time. It was like that last night."

"In that case, I think I know what we must do, but I will have to ask for your assistance once again, Lady Marianne."

"Of course, I am happy to do anything to help rid the neighborhood of such a villain," Marianne replied without any hesitation. "Only tell me what you have in mind."

CHAPTER 30

Late that evening, Marianne was doing her best to keep up an appearance of cheerful calm, but as the minutes ticked by, she felt increasingly that it was an impossible task. She could not imagine how Captain Larkin was able to stand the waiting that made up his part of the scheme, for he would have absolutely nothing to distract himself with. *She*, at least, was thoroughly occupied by entertaining Daphne and Elizabeth.

Daphne had been delighted when Marianne returned home with Elizabeth, explaining that she had brought the girl home to spend the night and keep them company while Lord Sedgewick was away. Elizabeth had been sternly cautioned against breathing a word of the recent events to Daphne, and she seemed perfectly capable of keeping her lips sealed. Indeed, Marianne found herself impressed with the child's fortitude as they whiled away the evening with music in the conservatory.

The girls were sleeping now, Marianne was relieved to see as she slipped into their chamber to check on them. Moonlight spilled across their sweet, relaxed faces, and she moved to the window to adjust the curtains. Gazing out into the night, she could not help but turn her eyes in the direction of the Larkin home, although of course it was not possible to see it from her vantage point. Somewhere over there, though, she knew Captain Larkin was crouched in readiness, concealed in the sturdy wardrobe in Elizabeth's usual chamber.

Marianne had helped to make up Elizabeth's bed herself before leaving with the little girl, and she was confident that the cushions and pillows were arranged convincingly enough to fool anyone into thinking they were a sleeping child. Especially once darkness fell, and especially with the crowning flourish of the unassuming doll flung carelessly on the foot of the bed. *La Fumèe*, should he try to search the child's chamber a second night in a row, could scarcely miss that prize. Marianne only hoped for Captain Larkin's sake that the spy *did* dare to enter the room, for otherwise he would be spending a very cramped and dull night for no reason.

It was a clever bit of misdirection, for no one watching the doctor's home could know that Elizabeth was not there. Marianne had chosen to smuggle the girl into a carriage rather than risk walking back home and perhaps being observed. It was nerve-wracking to think that someone was monitoring their movements, and she could not rid herself of an uncomfortable prickling feeling along her neck anytime she thought of it.

If all went according to plan, however, Captain Larkin would soon be leaping out of the wardrobe and detaining the wretched spy. Then perhaps she could avoid seeing the object of her affections for a very long time. It might take an entire lifetime before her heart stopped aching for him, now that she had fully acknowledged to herself how desperately she cared for the man. But it would surely be a little easier if she were not in such close and constant proximity.

Marianne had had years of experience with Daphne's ability to mimic sound sleep in order to get into some mischief while the house was silent, and had gone to check on the girls. Well satisfied the two were truly sleeping and not merely feigning, Marianne left the bedchamber and turned down the passageway to her own. It seemed highly unlikely that she would be able to sleep, but she supposed it would be best to at least make an attempt.

She had just passed the threshold of her own bedchamber when some faint sound had her pausing in her tracks. Glancing back, however, she saw it was only one of the maids, the new one, whose name escaped her at the moment, with an apologetic expression on her face.

"Oh, you startled me," Marianne laughed, feeling foolish.

"I beg your pardon, my lady, I know I ought not be wandering about the halls so late. I couldn't sleep, so I thought to fetch some mending to work on. There's no sense in wasting the hours, after all," the girl said sheepishly.

"Of course, that's perfectly alright. Carry on," said Marianne pleasantly, feigning a yawn. "I don't believe I can keep my eyes open for another minute, myself."

She closed her chamber door behind her, the benign smile slipping instantly from her face as her mind raced furiously. As a precaution, she walked rather noisily over to her bed and made as much racket as she could with moving the coverlet and laying down, then slipping soundlessly back to the doorway. Sure enough, there was a shadow along the bottom of the door, just as if someone were standing there listening to her movements.

The girl's story was plausible enough, she supposed, but something in her tone or expression was just slightly wrong. It was something Marianne could not quite put a finger on, but could not ignore, either. She was new to the household, and to the area as well. The housekeeper had mentioned something about the girl wanting to take the place to be nearer to an elderly relative, Marianne was fairly certain.

It was true that no one had seen Elizabeth leaving the Larkin home, but Marianne reflected with dawning horror that of course the staff of the Sedgewick estate were privy to that information. What if *la Fumèe* had managed to slip an agent into her staff, a ridiculously easy a task, given the fractured state of the staff lately. He would have no difficulty in gaining access to the home at night. And he would certainly be privy to the information that Elizabeth was here now, rather than safely in her own bed. Captain Larkin would be waiting all night for nothing, Marianne realized, for the spy would soon be searching *this* home.

The idea of the evil and dangerous man slipping into the chamber with the innocently sleeping girls filled her with fury. She had to order herself to stay still and silent for several long moments. Finally, the shadow moved away from her door, and she could hear soft footsteps trailing down the corridor. There was no way to possibly get word to Captain Larkin in time, and Marianne realized she was going to have to rely on herself and no one else.

Scarcely daring to breathe, she eased her door open a bit to peer into the shadowy passage beyond. She could just barely make out the form of the duplicitous maid, moving steadily towards a room at the end of the corridor. Of course, Marianne understood suddenly, because that particular room possessed a balcony which anyone nimble enough might climb up to. The door leading to the balcony was kept locked for that very reason, but the maid was undoubtedly about to remove *that* barrier.

Seeing no other option, Marianne waited until the maid had entered the far room, then raced as quietly as she possibly could to Daphne's bedchamber. She forced herself to open and close the door slowly, so as to not awaken the girls or alert the maid, then looked frantically about the room for some sort of weapon.

Blessing Daphne and her unconventional pursuits, she spotted a fencing foil. Marianne could not claim any sort of proficiency with the weapon, but it possessed the merit of being quite sharp, for Daphne would scarcely deign to practice with a blunted foil. She snatched it up and crouched beside the bed, hoping the shadows covered her, just as the chamber door swung silently open.

It was a wonder the spy did not hear her pounding heartbeat, Marianne thought, as the noise thundered in her own ears. The shape of a man was outlined in the doorway for a long moment, and then it began moving closer to the bed. The maid was nowhere in sight, having fulfilled her obligations, Marianne supposed, and *la Fumèe* slipped noiselessly from one object to another, intent upon his mission.

Marianne had almost begun to hope that he would abandon the attempt without disturbing the children, and then she could send for Captain Larkin to detain the maid and find out the rest of the spy's plans. Unfortunately, Daphne shifted in her sleep just then, and the faint light revealed her own doll, which she still clutched most nights despite her insistence that she was beyond all childish things. The spy hissed out a breath at the sight, and Marianne knew that she would have to confront him. Just as he reached out a scarred hand towards the bed, she stood up from her crouching position, the foil poised menacingly at his throat.

"Do not touch her," she ordered as sternly as she could manage in a hushed tone, her fingers clenched desperately on the handle of the weapon. "Or I will run this blade straight though you."

CHAPTER 31

"Oh, surely not my lady," whispered the man roughly. "Think of the dreadful mess that would make. Blood all over the sleeping children, you know. They might never recover from the shock."

"I will take my chances. There is nothing here for you and you *will* stop terrorizing this poor child. Leave now and you may save your miserable life."

He laughed softly. "Do you have any idea the sheer power it takes to run a man through? The precision? Unless the aim is just right, the blade will be deflected by the ribs, and woe to you if I do not die," he said viciously.

With her own heart beating rapidly in her chest, she considered his words. She knew he was right. She had learned those facts when she had made her little foray into medicine and anatomy., but she would not leave her sister and Elizabeth to the man's mercy. She had to try. "Just leave," she hissed, praying that he would go and leave them in peace.

"I have never in my life admitted defeat and I am certainly not about to do so now just because a trembling girl makes threats she cannot possibly keep," he snapped, his voice raising enough to wake the sleeping children.

Elizabeth, opening her eyes to such a scene, let out a shriek that distracted Marianne for an instant. The spy took advantage of that moment and knocked the foil violently from Marianne's hand. Defenseless, she flung herself in front of the girls all the while knowing that it was an act of futility. She could sense the desperation in the man, and she had no doubt that he would kill them all rather than risk exposure and failure. She would not, however, go down without a fight, and perhaps she might buy Daphne and Elizabeth enough time to escape.

"Run." she snarled, amazing herself at the feral sound ripping its way from her throat as she pushed the girls toward the door. She then launched herself at the intruder, her only goal to slow and distract him. She was hardly surprised when he shook her away quite easily, but it *was* a shock when he promptly slid limply to the floor. Gasping for breath, she looked up to see Captain Larkin with a heavy brass candlestick still raised in one hand.

"Oh, good, you figured it out," she managed to say before he dropped the candlestick and snatched her into his arms.

"Marianne, are you hurt? Are you alright?" Captain Larkin demanded, holding her at arm's length for a moment over the prone form of the groaning spy. His eyes searched her face for any sign of serious injury and then clasped her suddenly to his hard chest as Doctor Larkin and a small crowd of servants came rushing in with lights.

"I am perfectly fine," she whispered, knowing that her breathlessness and racing pulse had as much to do with his embrace as with the violent altercation that had just taken place.

"You are indeed perfect," he murmured, pulling her close once more and holding her against the length of him.

She looked up at him, wanting to say something, to express her thanks perhaps, but he did not let a word escape her lips. He was suddenly kissing her, his mouth hot and insistent upon hers. If possible the rapid beating of her heart increased tenfold.

"Really, now, Andrew," interrupted the voice of Doctor Larkin, at least, Marianne assumed it was, for everything beyond Captain Larkin was relegated to a vague buzzing. "This is the sort of impulsive behavior that either results in a scandal or a marriage."

"As that marriage has been my fondest wish for a great while now," the captain said, looking intently into Marianne's eyes as he answered his brother. "I fear I am unable to regret my impulse much, unless it displeases the lady." He tipped her face up to his with a finger under her chin. "What say you, my lady? Are you displeased?"

"I have no protest to make," Marianne laughed, feeling suddenly and ridiculously happy. Captain Larkin seemed to be on the point of kissing her once again, but *la Fumèe* made a rather loud noise of protest as his consciousness returned, and the sound recalled the captain to his other purpose, and he temporarily released his hold on Marianne.

IT WAS NEARLY DAWN BEFORE THE EXCITEMENT IN THE household fully died down, and she had caught a scant handful of hours of sleep since then, but Marianne had never felt more alert in her life than she did the following afternoon. Elizabeth and Daphne had fallen back asleep shortly after teatime, and Arabella and Ellen were sitting in the drawing room eagerly discussing the events that they had missed.

Captain Larkin had left for the nearest military post with *la Fumèe* and the unfortunate maid. The spy and his accomplice were both trussed hand and foot, then chained to the carriage door as a further precaution, as *la Fumèe* was notorious for his ability to escape restraints. In all likelihood, the captain would be gone at least until the next day, and even that short span of time seemed an interminable delay to Marianne. She felt too energized to sit quietly with Arabella and Ellen, although they had not exhausted their questions for her by any means, and so was passing by the window just as Captain Larkin rode unexpectedly up the drive. Unable to wait even the few minutes that it would take him to dismount and come inside, she rushed impulsively out to greet the man she had been in love with since she was a child.

He was just striding up the steps, windblown and looking more ridiculously handsome than ever when she burst through the doorway. For one terrifying instant she was struck by the sudden fear that he might regret his impulsive action and statement of the previous night, that it had all been a by-product of an exciting and dramatic situation. The brilliant smile that lit up his entire visage when he laid eyes upon her, however, dispelled that fear immediately.

"I returned as quickly as I could," he announced, crossing the remaining distance in a few long steps. "I could hardly bear to be away from you for a single hour."

"It would have been inviting trouble to try and keep *la Fumèe* prisoner here for any length of time, I suppose," Marianne replied understandingly. She could afford to be generous, after all, since he had returned a full day sooner than she had expected.

"Ordinarily I would not mind inviting trouble, particularly, but I have far more interesting things on my mind at the moment than mere international espionage rings. Tell me, truly, Lady Marianne, are you displeased that you must marry me?"

"What if I said that I was?" asked Marianne teasingly. "Would you graciously accept my decision?"

"Not in the least, I am afraid. I have already turned my back on my strongest resolutions, rejected the most fascinating commission I could ever dream of, and begun plotting out various campaigns of convincing you that you ought to marry myself rather than that confounded brilliant scholar. If you do not wish to marry me, I must tell you that I will respect your decision and devote the rest of my life, should it take so long, to persuading you to change your mind, and I must tell you, I am most diligent in my campaigns."

He looked quite fierce as he spoke, one hand curling possessively around her waist, and Marianne felt a thrill at the idea of being so thoroughly persuaded.

"That sounds rather delightful, but I must confess it will be sadly unnecessary," she admitted. "I have always wanted to marry you, which I suppose is not the sort of information I ought to give so freely, as it may go to your head. It is the truth, however, and I have already declined poor Sir Henry's proposal."

"I will never be as clever as you, or as brilliant as you," he said. "But there are some things I think I can teach you." His eyes shone with passion, and she licked her lips eagerly.

"I shall be your most enraptured student," she said, as he pulled her into his arm.

You cannot begin to imagine how much I love you," he murmured, kissing her triumphantly.

"I suspect it is a great deal," she replied once she had caught her breath again. "But tell me what you meant just now, about turning down a fascinating commission. Whatever does that have to do with anything?"

"Oh, well, it is not important," he said a little sheepishly. "My mother, she arrives tomorrow, and she will be utterly delighted to meet you, by the way—"

"You will not succeed in distracting me by scaring me, sir," Marianne interrupted drily.

"It was worth the attempt. However, she has always taken a great dislike to my taking dangerous commissions and has done her best to use her considerable influence to keep me from them. I succeed about half of the time in finding my way into action despite her, but lately she has blocked me at every turn. I have been despairing of my options. Earlier this week I finally received one that sounded promising. It is in Egypt, which has always fascinated me, but I declined it. Partly for Elizabeth's sake, for I did take to heart what you said to me. I cannot drag the child willy-nilly around the globe, but in all honesty, it was because I could not very well propose to you under such circumstances. I have several very tame domestic options, or I can resign from the service altogether if you would prefer, for nothing in the world matters to me so much as your happiness."

"That is so thoroughly…ridiculous," concluded Marianne, rather unexpectedly, it seemed, for the captain blinked at her in some surprise. "I hope you can rescind your letter declining that post, for I have *always* wanted to travel to Egypt, and I will be furious to miss such an opportunity. Elizabeth will love it, too, I am certain."

"Do you really mean that?" Captain Larkin demanded, looking at her in amazement.

"Of course, I do. I imagine you would languish away in an environment devoid of adventure just as much as I would without books. I would never think to ask such a thing of you any more than you would ask it of me. Really, if you think about it, it is a very logical pairing. I am sure I can find something new to study anywhere you might be called to go, and Elizabeth, well, she has already proven to be a very resilient girl."

"I know I've said it before, but you are the most fascinating creature," he replied after a moment, shaking his head in disbelief at his good fortune and then taking her in his arms once more.

"Fascinating," she said laying a finger upon his lips. "You have no idea."

"I think I shall soon learn," he said eye twinkling.

"Yes," she said, and pulled his face down to resume another lesson in kissing.

ALSO BY ISABELLA THORNE

THE SEDGEWICK LADIES
LADY ARABELLA AND THE BARON
HEALING MISS MILLWORTH
LADY MARIANNE AND THE CAPTAIN

SPINSTERS OF THE NORTH
THE HIDDEN DUCHESS
THE MAYFAIR MAID

THE LADIES OF BATH
The Duke's Daughter ~ Lady Amelia Atherton
The Baron in Bath ~ Miss Julia Bellevue
The Deceptive Earl ~ Lady Charity Abernathy
Winning Lady Jane ~ A Christmas Regency Romance
The Ladies of Bath Collection

THE LADIES OF LONDON
Wager on Love ~ Lady Charlotte

THE LADIES OF THE NORTH
The Duke's Winter Promise ~ A Christmas Regency Romance
The Viscount's Wayward Son
The Marquess' Rose

The Hawthorne Sisters

The Forbidden Valentine ~ Lady Eleanor

The Baggington Sisters

The Countess and the Baron ~ Prudence

Almost Promised ~ Temperance

The Healing Heart ~ Mercy

The Lady to Match a Rogue ~ Faith

※

Other Novels by Isabella Thorne

The Mad Heiress and the Duke ~ Miss Georgette Quinby

The Duke's Wicked Wager ~ Lady Evelyn Evering

Short Stories by Isabella Thorne

Colonial Cressida and the Secret Duke ~ A Short Story

Jane's Christmas Baby

Love Springs Anew

The Mad Heiress' Cousin and the Hunt

Mischief, Mayhem and Murder: A Marquess of Evermont

Mistletoe and Masquerade ~ 2-in-1 Short Story Collection

New Year's Masquerade

Stitched in Love

Collections by Isabella Thorne

Winter Holiday Collection

NEXT BOOK IN THE SEDGEWICK LADIES SERIES

Lady Daphne Sedgewick, youngest daughter of the Earl of Ashbury and her friend Miss Elizabeth Southhampton took a few moments to compare experiences and catch their breath together in a rather secluded alcove that would certainly have made an excellent place for clandestine assignations, concealing as it was. This fact was demonstrated only a few minutes after the two girls had taken their seats, when a small cluster of young ladies paused near the sheltering potted palms and began a frankly indiscrete conversation.

Eyes wide with surprise and suppressed amusement, Daphne and Elizabeth listened shamelessly as the unknown girls discussed various gentry with a sort of gleeful malice that they would surely have never dared express openly. As most of the unknowing victims were people that Daphne and Elizabeth had only met that evening – if at all – the majority of the conversation really revealed more about the speakers than their subjects.

Daphne was just beginning to grow bored with the unvarying gossip, and was toying with the idea of fabricating a cough or sneeze in order to scare the girls away, when the mention of Lord Edmund St. James caught her interest.

"St. James is here, looking more handsome than ever," said one young lady, her shrill voice sounding rather bitter as she spoke the name. "And from all accounts his fortune is even greater. It is his unpleasant disposition, then, that must deter all the young ladies."

"I do not recall that his disposition was much of a deterrent to *you* last Season, when you were so terribly determined to catch his eye," her companion replied, evidently happy to needle the other when the chance presented itself. "Yet that goal certainly seemed to fall by the wayside anyhow."

"I could hardly know how unpleasant his disposition was at the outset, could I?" retorted the other girl tartly. "Such a thing may be concealed on a superficial acquaintance, but never for very long. I assure you that once I understood how unpleasant a gentleman St. James truly is, I did not waste another second of my time on him – and a good thing, too, or else I might not have captured the attentions of my own Mr. Greenly. I daresay all of these young country ladies coming out for their first Season will make the same discovery as I did before too much longer and move along to more favorable pastures."

"His fortune is great enough that more than a few of their doting mamas will instruct them to turn a blind eye to his failings as a companion, I should imagine. I never saw such a crop of unrefined little creatures!"

"I daresay you are right – they will be throwing themselves at him shockingly before the night is finished," remarked a third lady, who had been doing more listening than speaking up to that point. "Not that it will do them any good. Lord Edmund St. James could have been married dozens of times, unpleasant disposition aside, but he has never shown the slightest interest in anyone to my knowledge. It is a source of great distress to his family, from what I understand, for he is the sole son and heir, and the fortune may pass away from them altogether if he does not marry and produce an heir in good time. I have it on good authority that his parents have absolutely demanded that he find a fiancée this very season."

"What unfortunate timing, Sarah, you might have had him after all – but for your understanding with Mr. Greenly," laughed the second lady unkindly. "That, as you have given us to understand so many times, is practically iron-clad. I wonder who the Lord St. James will deign to favor out of the remaining young ladies?"

"It will hardly be anyone who is too obviously in want of a rich husband," mused her friend, who was evidently ignoring the jibe with great deliberation. "*Those* girls are always far too obvious to catch a truly wealthy gentleman. Oh, what a thoughtless remark! I do not include *you* in my observation, of course, dear! If I were to venture a guess, I should say that outrageous country bumpkin in the yellow silk will pursue St. James most ferociously. Her family is in no need of a fortune, and she appears to have a rather small regard for decorum."

Elizabeth began to make an indignant squeak at this unkind description of Daphne, but Daphne quelled her with a ferocious glance. She wanted to hear what else would be said.

"Who, Daphne Sedgewick? I would hardly describe her as a bumpkin," the third lady demurred. "She is certainly a great beauty, and you are quite right in saying that her family is in no need of a fortune, for both of her older sisters have made excellent matches and her father is an earl. She is decidedly vivacious and lively; I will grant you that. If she sets her sights on Lord St. James as all the other girls do when first making their debuts, he had better resign himself at once, for I daresay he will not be able to withstand such an onslaught."

"Especially not if he is being pressed to take a wife quickly – a certain disregard for propriety would really be expedient in such a scenario."

For a moment Daphne felt stricken, mortified at the idea that she had somehow inadvertently made such an impression on her very first foray into London society. But almost at once she discredited the thought. These were three evil-minded harpies, not interested in anything other than slandering the people they envied and slipping thinly veiled insults to one another. Their assessment of her character could hardly be considered unbiased. Tossing her head, she spoke quite loudly to Elizabeth.

"Dear me, did you ever see anything so pitiful as the aging spinsters at this ball? I quite admire their strength and courage in coming to events night after night, year after year, always hoping to finally find an acceptable gentleman willing to save them from a fate of old-maidenhood."

"Oh, indeed, it is enough to break your heart," agreed Elizabeth earnestly, also pitching her voice to carry clearly. "One cannot even really mind it when they attempt to make cutting remarks, the poor things, and inevitably sound only bitter and spiteful."

"You are right – it is terribly difficult to feel anything besides pity for such transparently desperate attempts," Daphne said, letting her voice drip with sorrowful condescension.

There was a trio of outraged gasps from the other side of the potted palm trees, accompanied by a rather frantic rustle of fabric as the three hapless ladies made haste to remove themselves. Daphne only hesitated for a moment before deciding to satisfy their horrified curiosity, and stepped boldly out of the alcove to make deliberate eye contact with her critics.

She saw at once that her barely informed insults had hit with devastated precision, for all three were ladies who could scarcely claim the term 'young' any longer. Aside from flushes of shock and surprise, they were all rather faded and pale, each clearly attempting to conceal any natural maturity and thereby inadvertently enhancing the march of years. It did not help, of course, that their faces seemed inclined from years of habit into lines of contempt and bitterness.

Daphne said nothing, instead sweeping her eyes over the women with expression of disdain fairly emanating from her being. She could sense Elizabeth standing by her side, doubtless braced for whatever form her friend's fury would take. Before Daphne - or any of the three ladies who stood frozen in dismay and anger before her – could decide upon a course of action, however, Lord Edmund St. James himself approached, his striking green eyes fixed directly on Daphne.

With a small pang of regret, for she really had found the gentleman interesting and pleasant, Daphne deliberately turned her back on Lord St. James and strode off in the opposite direction, a cut that could not be mistaken for anything else.

"I suppose you felt simply honor-bound to do the precise opposite of throwing yourself at Lord St. James," Elizabeth said. "It hardly seemed fair to the man, when he really had done nothing to deserve such an insult as far as either of us knows."

"Perhaps it is unfair, but I can hardly hold a conversation with him when everyone is assuming I have set my sights on him," Daphne said with a shrug, wishing that she did not feel a pang at the glimpse of wounded surprise that she had caught in Lord St. James' eyes when she whirled away from him so rudely.

Order your copy at Amazon: The Earl's Broken Heart

Continue Reading for a Sneak Peek of….

The Duke's Daughter ~ Lady Amelia Atherton
Ladies of Bath, Book 1
By Isabella Thorne

A Duke's Daughter and a Navy Commander …a tragic accident, a secret cypher, and a clandestine engagement. A strange twist of Fate brought the unlikely pair together… now nothing will keep them apart.

Lady Amelia Atherton is not a woman to be trifled with. Known as the diamond of the Ton, she is beautiful, witty, and the only daughter of the Duke of Ely. The men of the Peerage see her as a prize to be won, and perhaps a way to obtain her father's influence.

Commander Samuel Beresford is the brash, sometimes rude, younger son, of the Earl of Blackburn. A Royal Navy Commander who has little time for the affectations of Society.

Two people have never been so mismatched, but when Amelia's father, The Duke of Ely, dies under mysterious circumstances, and Samuel's elder brother is poisoned within a mere day of the Duke's death, both Lady Amelia and Commander Beresford find themselves forced to work together in a desperate search for the culprit.

Amelia was always careful to guard her feelings, that is until she met Samuel Beresford. Now everything Lady Amelia once took for granted has been shattered, and with the Dukedom in the hands of her odious Uncle Declan, Amelia and Samuel plan an elaborate ruse, in the hope of drawing out the murderer.

Lady Amelia Atherton considered herself as tough as a diamond, but somehow Samuel Beresford has found his way into her heart…

Neither could imagine falling in love … now it seems they cannot imagine loving anyone else.

Enjoy the Entire
The Ladies of Bath Collection
By Isabella Thorne

Collection Includes:
The Duke's Daughter
The Baron in Bath
The Deceptive Earl

THE DUKE'S DAUGHTER

With a few lines of black ink scrawled on cream parchment, her life had changed forever. Lady Amelia had to say goodbye, but she could not bear to. She sat alone in the music room contemplating her future. Outside the others gathered, but here it was quiet. The room was empty apart from the piano, a lacquered ash cabinet she had received as a gift from her father on her twelfth birthday. She touched a key and the middle C echoed like the voice of a dear friend. The bench beneath her was the same one she had used when she begun learning, some ten years ago, and was as familiar to her as her father's armchair was to him.

Lighter patches on the wood floor marked where the room's other furniture had sat for years, perhaps for as long as she had been alive. New furnishings would arrive, sit in different places, make new marks, but she would not be here to see it. Amelia ran her fingers across the keys, not firmly enough to make a sound, but she heard the notes in her head regardless. When all her world was turmoil, music had been a constant comforting presence. Turmoil. Upheaval. Chaos. What was the proper word for her life now?

She breathed in a calming breath, and smoothed her dark skirt, settling it into order. She would survive; she would smile again, but first, she thought, she would play. She would lose herself in the music, this one last time.

Two Weeks Earlier

Lady Amelia looked the gentleman over. Wealthy, yes, but not enough to make up for his horrid appearance. *That* would take considerably more than mere wealth. He leered at her as though she were a pudding he would like to sample. Though it was obvious he was approaching to ask her to dance, she turned on her heel in an unmistakable gesture and pretended to be in deep conversation with her friends. Refusing the man a dance outright would be gauche, but if her aversion was apparent enough before the man ever asked, it would save them both an embarrassment. She smoothed her rich crimson gown attempting to project disinterest. It was a truly beautiful garment; silk brocade with a lush velvet bodice ornamented with gold and pearl accents.

Lady Charity, one of Amelia's friends in London, smiled, revealing overly large teeth. The expression exaggerated the flaw, but Charity had other attributes.

"That is an earl you just snubbed," said Charity, wide-eyed. It both galled and delighted Lady Charity the way Amelia dismissed gentlemen. Lady Amelia did not approve of the latter, she did not take joy in causing others discomfort. It was a necessity, not a sport.

"Is he still standing there looking surprised?" Amelia asked, twirling one of her golden ringlets back into place with the tip of a slender gloved finger. Looking over her shoulder to see for herself would only confuse the man into thinking she was playing coy. "I am the daughter of a duke, Charity. I need not throw myself at every earl that comes along."

"Thank goodness, or you would have no time for anything else." Charity's comment bore more than a tinge of jealousy.

Lady Amelia's debut earlier this Season had drawn the attention of numerous suitors, and the cards still arrived at her London townhouse in droves. Each time she went out, whether to a ball or to the Park, she was inundated with tireless gentlemen. If she were a less patient woman, it would have become tedious. Gracious as she was, Amelia managed to turn them all down with poise. Lady Amelia's father, the Duke of Ely, was a kind man who doted on his only daughter but paid as little mind to her suitors as Amelia herself; always saying there was plenty of time for such things. Her debut like most aspects of her upbringing was left to the professionals. What do I pay tutors for? He had said, when a younger Amelia had asked him a question on the French verbs. There had been many tutors. Amelia had learned the languages, the arts, the histories, music and needlepoint until she was, by Society's standards, everything a young woman should be. She glanced across the hall to that same father, and found him deep in conversation with several white haired men, no doubt some of the older lords talking politics as they were wont to do. She flashed him a quick smile and he toasted her with his glass.

Father had even indulged her by hiring a composer to teach her the piano, after she proven herself adept and eager to learn. If any of these flapping popinjays were half the man her father was…she thought with irritation.

Lady Patience, the less forward of Lady Amelia's friends, piped in, "Men are drawn to your beauty like moths to a flame." Her voice had a sad quality to it.

"I'm sure you will find the perfect beau, Patience." Amelia replied.

"Yes, well, you might at least toss them our way, when you have decided against them." Charity said. She peeked wide eyed over her silvered fan which covered her bosom with tantalizing art. Amelia's eyes were brought back to her friends and she smiled.

While Charity was blonde and buxom, Patience was diminutive, yet cursed with garish red hair. The wiry, unruly locks had the habit of escaping whatever style her maid attempted, leaving the girl looking a bit like a waif. Although her dress was a lovely celestial blue frock trimmed round the bottom with lace and a white gossamer Polonese long robe joined at the front with rows of satin beading, she still appeared frazzled and misplaced at an elegant ball like the one they were attending.

Charity's flaws were more obvious, apart from her wide mouth. She had a jarring laugh, and wore necklines so low they barely contained her ample bosom. The gown she was wearing extenuated this feature with many rows of white scalloped lace and a rosy pink bodice clasped just underneath. It bordered on vulgar. Amelia intended to make the polite suggestion on their next shopping trip that Lady Charity perhaps should purchase an extra yard of fabric so she might have enough for an *entire* dress.

"Do not be foolish, Patience. You deserve someone wonderful. If we must be married, it should be to someone that… excites us," Amelia said, rising up onto her toes and clasping her hands in front of her breast.

Her comment caused Patience to flush with embarrassment. It was easy to forget Patience was two years older than Amelia and a year older than Charity, for her naivety gave her a childlike demeanor.

"Not all of us are beautiful enough to hold out for someone handsome," said Patience. When she blushed, her freckles blended with the rosiness of her cheeks. Her eyes alighted with hope, and she was pretty in a shy sort of way.

Charity nodded her agreement, but Amelia frowned and clasped Patience's hands. "You are sweet and bright and caring. Any man would be lucky to have you for his wife. Do not settle because you feel you have no choice. The right man will come along. Just you wait and see."

Tears swelled in Patience's bright blue eyes. Amelia hoped she would not begin to cry; the girl was prone to hysterics and leaps of emotion. Charity was only a notch better, and if one girl began the other was certain to follow. Two crying girls was not the spectacle Amelia hoped to make at a ball. She clapped her hands together and twirled around, so her skirts fanned out around her feet.

"Come now; let us find some of those handsome men to dance with. It should not be hard for three young ladies like us." Amelia glanced back. Patience was wiping at her eyes and fidgeting with her dress— no matter how many times Amelia scolded her for it, the girl could not quit the nervous and irritating gesture—which generally wrinkled her dress with two fist sized wads on either side of her waist. Meanwhile Charity was puffing out her chest like a seabird. One more deep breath and she was sure to burst her seams.

It would be up to Amelia, then. In a matter of minutes she had snagged two gentlemen and placed one with Charity and one with Patience on the promise that she herself would dance with them afterward. Though men waited around her, looking hopefully in her direction, none dared approach until she gave them a sign of interest. She had already earned a reputation of being discerning with whom she favored, and no man wanted the stigma of having been turned away. Amelia perused the ballroom at her leisure, silently wishing for something more than doters and flatterers after her father's influence.

❦

Samuel Beresford did not want to be here. He found balls a tremendous waste of time, the dancing and the flirting and, thinly veiled beneath it all, the bargaining. For that was what marriage boiled down to, a bargain. It was all about striking a deal where each person involved believed they had the advantage over the other. If it were not for his brother's pleading, he would never be seen at a fancy affair like this. Dressed in his naval uniform, a blue coat with gold epaulets and trimmings and white waistcoat and breeches, he attracted more attention than he wished.

"Stop scowling, Samuel," said Percival as he returned to his brother's side from a brief sojourn with a group of lords. "You look positively dour."

"Did you find the man?" Samuel inquired.

Percival sipped his wine and shook his head. "It is no matter. Let us concentrate on the women. We should be enjoying their company and you seem intent on scaring them all off with your sour expression."

Unlike himself, Samuel's older brother Percival loved the frivolity of these occasions. As the eldest son of an earl it was very nearly an obligation of his office to enjoy them, so Samuel could not begrudge his brother doing his duty.

"You think it my expression and not our looks that are to blame?" Samuel asked, only half in jest. To appease his brother he hid his scowl behind the rim of his wine glass.

The Beresford brothers were not of disagreeable appearance, but they lacked the boyish looks so favored at the moment. They did not look gentlemanly, the brothers were too large, their features too distinctly masculine, for the women to fawn and coo over. Additionally Samuel had been sent to the Royal Naval Academy at the age of twelve, a life that had led him to be solidly built, broad across the chest and shoulders. He felt a giant amongst the gentry.

"Smile a bit brother, and let us find out." Percy elbowed Samuel in the side.

"What is a wife but an ornament to show off at these functions? I cannot imagine any necessary criteria other than beauty. Just pick the prettiest one and have done with it." Samuel's comment earned him a narrow-eyed glare from a passing woman. He smiled gaily back at her.

"How can I when my brother insists on offending them before I can open my mouth? I should have left you at home," Percy said with a long suffering sigh.

"I wish you would have done."

Samuel did not mind life ashore in small doses. It was a chance to have a real meal, something other than salt-cured meat, and a decent cup of tea with fresh cream. He also got to spend time with Percy, though he would not admit to missing his brother out loud. After too long on land, however, he become irritated and itched to get back to his ship, until it became a near-physical pain to be away from it.

"Father insisted you interact with women whose company you did not pay for." Percy said as he sipped from his wine glass.

"I heard him threatening to reduce your allowance. Do you think you could survive on your officer's stipend?"

"I could," Samuel said peevishly.

"Besides, I have missed you, dear brother and if I did not drag you along with me I would never get to see you," said Percy. "No doubt you will be back at sea before the week is out."

Until the time Samuel had joined the Royal Navy and left home, he and his brother had been nigh inseparable. Only a year separated them in age, but the lives they led could not have been more different. Samuel had long ago banished any remnants of jealousy he had once felt at his brother's status, something earned with nothing more than the luck of being born first, and Samuel would no more trade places with Percy than he would with a beggar on the street.

"I shall be a good little brother then and assist you in your hunt for a wife," said Samuel. "After all it is essential that the heir get an heir. I myself am not so encumbered." He swapped his empty glass for a full one and walked in a lazy circle around the room, his brother in tow.

"First, we must find the most beautiful woman in the room. No, not her, that is for certain. Did you see the ears on that one? I could use them for wings and fly myself to France."

Percy snickered, but turned it into a cough behind his hand. "Really now Samuel, stop insulting them and be serious!"

It was Samuel's opinion that Percy would benefit from considerably less seriousness in his life. He already bore the marks of stress and duty in the frown lines beside his mouth and even a few strands of grey had appeared in his dark hair.

"Fine, fine," said Samuel, coming to a halt. He never felt quite steady on solid ground and was always bracing himself for the rocking of a deck. "There. She is the one."

Samuel pointed. Percy swatted his hand down and looked around anxiously. "Do not go pointing like you have seen something you wish to buy in a shop window. These sorts of women do not appreciate being treated so. And no, certainly not her," Percival hissed.

Percival was being obstinate. The woman was clearly the most lovely in the room by a fair margin. She had hair the color of warm honey and her gown was a vibrant red, which perfectly complemented the pearly sheen of her skin. Luminescent that is what she was, shining in the light of the chandelier.

"Why not?" Samuel asked, frowning. He squinted, trying to pick out some flaw his brother must be seeing.

"Because she" said Percy, taking Samuel by the arm and drawing him further away from the lady in question, "is Lady Amelia Atherton."

"Lady Amelia? What luck! You do know my ship's name is the *Amelia*, Percy. You cannot count this as anything but fate that you should marry her." Privately, Samuel did not believe in fate, but his brother was a romantic. The sooner he got his brother a bride, the sooner he could quit these ghastly outings.

Percy was gaping at Samuel as if he were a fool. "While you may find that a fine reason to select a wife, it is not a matter of whether or not *I* will have *her*. She is most sought after woman of the Season. Beautiful, wealthy, the daughter of the Duke of Ely; I will just step in line behind her hundred other suitors, shall I?"

Though Percy had lived a charmed life, he had never acquired the arrogance or confidence of some of his peers, to his detriment.

"Do not step in line behind them, dear brother. March to the front. Women like a little brashness."

"How many drinks have you had, Samuel? It would do nothing but embarrass me to treat my peers rudely."

"Damn. Why would you care what they think?"

"I am in Lords with the lot of them. I won't make enemies without cause. No, pick another, any other," Percy insisted. He had gone a little pale, as if the mere thought of asking Lady Amelia Atherton for anything at all horrified him.

"This is all a bit absurd, do you not think, Percival? You are a man grown. She is hardly more than a girl. The right mix of good looks and bravado would have her melting in your arms," Samuel argued. "I cannot believe you are being unmanned by a girl of what, eight and ten?"

"Do you see the swarm of men about her? Men who have tried, and failed, to do just as you seem to think I should do with ease. Count me out, Samuel," said Percy. "Besides, having a wife quite so beautiful is asking for a lifetime of headaches."

Samuel had no firsthand experience with wives, but he could not imagine handling one was any more challenging than handling a ship. Spirited, willful, but under the right command, pliable and eager to serve. He told Percy as much.

"Oh really, *Commander?*" said Percy, brow furrowed in the way that meant he was trying to hold back laughter. "If you are so skilled at 'taming the willful seas' let us see you manage a single dance out of her."

"Me?" said Samuel, poking himself in the chest. "I have no desire for a wife."

"But if you demonstrate these skills, perhaps I can learn from you. Go on now, what are you frightened of? For a man with your looks and… what was it, bravado? She should be sweet butter in your hands."

The challenge held little appeal for Samuel. She was pleasing to look at, but he would get nothing more from her than a dance, which was hardly worth his while.

Still, if it would demonstrate to his insecure brother than confidence was the crux of the matter, it would be worth it.

"Fine," said Samuel at last. He drained his glass and handed it off to Percy. With a hand through his already disheveled locks, he said, "Watch and learn, brother; though she will be ruined for you, once she has met me."

"Samuel, you cannot," Percy argued looking for a place to set down the two glasses he now held. "You are not introduced." He took a long suffering breath as if steeling himself. "Come, I will introduce you."

"You will not; you will ruin everything," Samuel said as he headed straight for the woman.

※

PERCY STOOD OPEN MOUTHED, BUT WATCHED WITH AVID interest and not-quite-hidden horror as Samuel marched over to the Lady Amelia Atherton. She was turned away at the moment, conversing with another gentleman. Samuel stepped up beside her, a step closer than the other man, just inside the amount of space considered polite, and the other man quite naturally backed up. Her hazel eyes flashed, and Percival half-expected her to slap his brother.

"Dear God man, you are boring the woman to death; can you not see that? Now run along," Samuel said, waving a dismissive hand at the fellow.

The man's look of outrage and befuddlement was quite the show, and Percival could barely keep from laughing aloud. He turned away a moment to compose himself, and when he turned back, his brother was bowing over the unfathomable Lady Amelia Atherton's hand. She had a look of bemusement on her face, her lips turned up in a slight smirk. Percival wondered just how long it would be until his brother was turned away with the same callousness that he had shown the previous man; although the next time, Percy supposed the dismissing would be done by the Lady Amelia.

WANT EVEN MORE REGENCY ROMANCE…

Follow Isabella Thorne on BookBub
https://www.bookbub.com/profile/isabella-thorne

❦

Sign up for my VIP Reader List!
at
https://isabellathorne.com/

Receive weekly updates from Isabella and an
EXCLUSIVE FREE STORY

❦

Like Isabella Thorne on Facebook
https://www.facebook.com/isabellathorneauthor/

Made in the USA
Las Vegas, NV
05 February 2025